HYPNOS

THE UNDERWORLD SAGA, BOOK SEVEN

Eva Pohler

Eva Pohler Books
20011 Park Ranch
San Antonio, Texas 78259
www.evapohler.com

Book Layout ©2017 BookDesignTemplates.com

Book Cover Design by B Rose Designz

Hypnos/ Eva Pohler. -- 1st ed.
Paperback ISBN 978-1-958390-41-2

For my sisters.

Contents

"What makes you think that dreams are any less real?"

--HYPNOS

<u>CHAPTER ONE</u>

Free Fall

Hypnos looked up at the sound of Jen screaming. She was falling through the air again, her blonde hair standing up like a candle flame. He rolled his eyes and said to her telepathically: *I love you, but you are the slowest learner I know.*

At the top of her voice, she screamed, "Catch me or I'll kill yooooo-ou!"

He shook his head. *You mean you'll* swallow *me. You can't* kill *me.*

"Eat me! I hate yoooooou!"

He laughed and darted from the tip of the boot of Italy up into the sky, catching her just before she would have plunged into the Ionian Sea.

"What is wrong with you?" she accused, breathing heavily in his arms. She narrowed her golden-brown eyes at him. "Do you take pleasure in my pain?"

Smiling, he said, "Well, yes, Babe. As a matter of fact..."

She slapped him. "This is serious. I'm never gonna get the hang of this if you don't start taking me seriously. It's been almost a year, and I still suck at flying."

He heaved a deep sigh. "Sorry. You're right. You're just so cute when you're flustered."

She was about to object when he kissed her. He wasn't sure if it would work and was prepared to be slapped again, but the corners of his mouth twitched into a smile when she quieted down and relaxed in his arms and—best of all—returned his kisses.

When he met her gaze, he frowned. Tears had formed in her eyes. "Babe? I'm the most thoughtless god alive. I'm truly sorry."

"What's taking me so long?" she asked. "I'll be riding Stormy forever at this rate."

"You have to believe in yourself," he said. "I don't think you actually believe you can fly."

She wiped the tears from her eyes and nodded.

Stormy flew up beside them and nuzzled Jen.

"What would I do without you, boy?" Jen said as she stroked his cheek.

Hip had an idea. "That's it. That's the answer."

Jen bent her brows. "Huh?"

"He's been your crutch. He's been holding you back."

The dark gray horse gave Hip an offended look—one that said, "Really? You can't be serious."

"He's been *helping* me." Jen crossed her arms. "If it weren't for him…"

"He's been great. Yes, I know. And I thank you for that, Stormy. But, listen, Jen. You should swear him off—just until you get the hang of flying solo."

"What?" Her face turned white. "Swear him off?"

"Don't allow yourself to ride him until you can fly on your own."

"But I've got so much going on right now—too many other things to try and get used to. Do you know how hard it is to witness the cruelty to children I see every single day?"

He kissed her nose. "Have I told you how proud I am of you?"

"Yeah right. I can't even fly. Therese could do it immediately. Her very first day."

"Because of her lucid dreaming."

"Huh?"

"She was already flying in the Dreamworld, so she knew what to do."

"Maybe I'm not meant to be a goddess. Have you ever wondered if you made a mistake, giving me your immortality? Then Therese had to give you *hers*, and then Than…"

"Nope. I believe you can do it." Hip tucked a golden strand behind her ear. "I know you can. Besides, in the ten months you've been the goddess of abused children, you've already done a lot of good."

"But there's only so much craziness…Did you know that Bobby looks up to Ares now like he's his new big brother?"

Hip frowned. "I guess I hadn't noticed."

"They're like two peas in a pod, and I'm just supposed to be okay with that. Has Ares given any thought to how hurt Bobby will be when he has to go back to Mount Olympus in a few days?"

"They're that close?"

"What part of *two peas in a pod* did you not understand?"

"It's just hard to imagine your little brother and the god of war hitting it off."

"Bobby can worm his way into anyone's heart. You remember how much Meg liked him, and Meg doesn't like anyone."

"I wouldn't go that far."

"Name one friend of hers, that's not a brother or sister."

"Well…" Hip could think of no one. Meg admired Athena, but he wouldn't say they were friends.

"See?"

"Where were you headed on Stormy when you fell?" Hip asked, wondering how much longer they should fly aimlessly above the sea.

"I was going to see Scylla."

Hip blanched. "What? Scylla? Are you crazy? Why?"

"Now, don't get mad…"

Every time she started a sentence with "Now, don't get mad," he braced himself, because it was usually something that made him very, very mad. "Spit it out."

"So, did you know that Scylla was abused by her parents?"

He did not like where Jen was going with this. "No."

"She said her mother was cruel to all of them because Keto believed it would make them stronger monsters."

"Looks like Keto was right."

"And Phorcys pretty much ignored everything, letting Keto make all the parenting decisions."

"I can see that."

"But Scylla didn't want to be a monster. Did you know that?"

"Apparently not."

"Circe transformed her into a beautiful girl for a while."

"Now that I knew."

"What? Do you think she was prettier than me?"

"Seriously? You're jealous of a giant crab serpent thingie with six heads and four eyes, not to mention that pack of dog heads around her waist?"

Jen scowled. "Anyway, when this merman, or someone Circe was crushing on, liked Scylla instead, Circe got jealous and changed Scylla back into a monster."

"And this is important to you because?"

"When Scylla was beautiful, her mother tried to kill her, and Scylla has never recovered from that."

"I still don't get how you fit into this story."

"Scylla reached out to me for help, and it's my duty to help her."

Hip arched a brow. "You don't really believe you can trust that monster, do you? It's probably a trap."

"Look. I know I can't fly. And I know I don't know everything yet about being a goddess. But I can recognize a fellow victim when I see one."

"You do remember what happened last summer in Circe's battle-field, right? You didn't just now suddenly get amnesia, did you? Scylla tried to kill us."

"Believe me. I remember. But Scylla and I are gonna make a deal."

Hip couldn't imagine how any deal with that monster could turn out good for Jen. "Babe, this is a dangerous time. You heard about the recent attack on Gaia, the giant that escaped, the mortals killed?"

"I know."

"Scylla could have been in on that."

"I don't think so. Didn't Apollo question Keto and Phorcys?"

"Yes, but…"

"Besides, a deal's a deal. She's gonna swear on the River Styx."

Hip sighed again, trying not to lose his patience. "What kind of deal?"

"Well, there's this little boy that's been praying to me. It took me a while to find him. He and dozens of other children are being abused by fishing companies in West Africa, in a place called Ghana."

"Abused how?" Hip turned toward Athens, happy to hold his wife in his arms as Stormy followed.

"Little children as young as two years old are sold into slavery by their own parents, who don't really know how badly their kids are treated. In fact, the parents are told their kids will be taken to school and be fed good meals and be better off with the fishing companies, but that's a big fat lie."

"What happens to them?" Hip asked.

"The kids are forced to work fourteen or more hours a day. The conditions are horrible. Their hands get all ripped up from trying to pull in the heavy nets. The worst part is when they're forced to dive into the lake to untangle the nets. So many kids have died doing that."

"Died?"

"Yeah. They get caught in the net, or get trapped beneath tree stumps, or get their eyes poked out by the branches."

"Oh, my gods." Hip shuddered.

"If they live, they aren't fed much or given time to rest. They sleep on the ground without bedding. And when they complain, they're thrown overboard. Sometimes they make it back on the boats, and sometimes they don't."

"Poor kids."

"Yeah. It's terrible. This one little boy is begging me to help him, because his older brother died and he has no one to watch over him. His master beats him with a stick full of thorns."

Hip loved Jen for wanting to help the children, but he was worried. "So, what's the deal with Scylla?"

"She's gonna help me bring down the fishing companies and save the children. In return, I'm gonna find Circe's beauty potion, give it to Scylla, and help her confront her mother."

"Oh, gods."

"Circe's place is abandoned, remember? She's in the Titan Pit. How hard can it be to find her stash?"

"She's got booby traps all over that place."

Jen's face fell. "Oh." Then she quickly added, "Well, it's worth the risk, if I can save all those children."

Hip's efforts to stop her crazy plan were interrupted when he received a telepathic summon from his father.

"Can we talk about this more later?" Hip asked her.

"Is Hades calling you, too?" she asked.

"Yeah. Climb on Stormy. Let's go."

They god-traveled to the stables to drop off Stormy and then went to Hades's main chambers.

When they entered the enormous jewel encrusted cavern that was his father's palace, Hip was alarmed by the look on his father's face. Below his curly dark hair, his blue eyes were somber, and the line of his mouth was grim.

"What is it?" Hip asked.

"Thanatos," Hades said. "The Maenads are coming for him."

Jen's face went pale. "But he's mortal. That will kill him, like, forever."

"Unless one of you takes his place," Hades said. "I'd do it myself if it weren't for the recent attacks on Gaia. I'm afraid I may be needed."

Hip agreed. They couldn't afford for one of the most powerful gods to be incapacitated for a week or two while his body recovered from the Maenads.

Hip recalled how painful it had been that terrible day when Zeus had chained him to a rock and had ordered an eagle to eat Hip's liver. He shuddered as he imagined how much worse it would feel to have his limbs and head violently ripped from his body.

But he couldn't let his brother die. The whole reason Thanatos had given up his immortality was so he could be a part of his mortal children's lives with Therese. It hadn't even been a year since Than had made the trade with Pete.

Standing on suddenly very weak knees, Hip said through a tight throat, "I'll do it."

Hades clapped a hand on Hip's shoulder. "I knew I could count on you, as much as I hate to put you through this. But there is one problem: The Maenads will hunt down Thanatos. They're locked onto his scent. You'll have to find a way to trick them into mistaking you for Than, or it won't work."

"But how in the world can I do that?" Hip asked.

"I'm not sure if it will work," Hades said. "But I have a plan."

CHAPTER TWO

The Maenads

Therese stood beneath one of two magnificent Elm trees outside of her aunt and uncle's log cabin in the San Juan Mountains of Colorado. Carol and Richard had invited her, Than, and the twins over for dinner, and since it was a beautiful summer's day, they'd decided to eat outside on the wooden deck. Four-year-old Lynn had taken only two bites of her hamburger and had scrambled out of her chair. Then the one-year-old twins, who had already been walking for two months, had wanted down from the table, too. Before any of the parents had been able to stop them, the twins had climbed the tree like two little monkeys.

"Hermie and Hestie, that's too high," Therese shouted from the ground below.

Therese's parents—two beautiful cardinals—flapped nervously around the upper branches, which were bouncing beneath the weight of the fearless babies.

Richard jumped from his chair. "Than, you better go up after them."

"They can speak in complete sentences AND climb like lemurs?" Carol wanted to know.

"They're going to fall and break something." Richard joined Therese beneath the tree, his black eyes full of worry.

Carol stood from her chair, too. "I've never seen anything like this before."

Therese frowned as Than climbed the tree toward the kids. They were perfectly capable of understanding their parents' commands. He shouldn't have to clamber up after them.

"You better mind your mother and come down this minute," Than said.

"Coming!" Hestie hollered.

In the next instant, the little girl was sailing through the air directly for Therese.

Carol screamed.

Therese's heart stopped beating for a moment as the air left her body. Because they traded fates with mortals, she and Thanatos didn't have any of the strength or demigod powers that their children possessed. She felt helpless as she held out her arms and caught her daughter. On impact, they fell to the ground.

After checking her daughter for injuries and seeing she was fine, she grabbed Hestie's arm and said, "Look at me. Don't you EVER do that again. Do you understand?"

"I'm sorry, Mommy. You said come down."

Carol rushed to them, her face nearly the same shade of red as her hair. "Is she alright?" She took Hestie into her arms. "No broken bones?"

Than climbed from the tree with Hermie clinging to his back.

Therese was grateful that at least one of the twins hadn't jumped.

These sticky situations were happening more and more frequently now that the twins were mobile. Therese wondered if she should come clean to her aunt and uncle and tell them the truth: Hermie and Hestie were not like other children. Would Carol and Richard be able to handle it?

Just then, Jen appeared riding on Stormy up to the back deck. She held a lead in one hand with Sugar on the end of it. Jen's face was as white as Sugar's coat.

"Jen!" Therese cried. "Is everything okay?"

"I need your help," she said. "Yours and Than's both. The horses got out of the pen today, and we need help rounding them up."

"We didn't even know you were in town," Carol said.

Than turned to Richard. "Do you mind watching the twins?"

"Of course not," Richard said. "You two go on."

Carol bounced Hestie in her arms. "Take as long as you need."

"Please listen to your Grammie and Grampie," Therese said to her children. "No more tree-climbing."

"Terry!" Lynn cried. "Don't go!"

Therese stepped into Stormy's stirrup and swung a leg behind Jen. "We'll be back soon, sweetie pie."

Than handed Hermie over to Richard and then mounted Sugar. "Be good kids. No adventures till we get back."

Once they were down the mountain on the dirt road, Therese asked, "What's really going on, Jen?" Therese had a bad feeling that Jen's problem had nothing to do with rounding up horses.

"We need to get away from your family," Jen said. "Let's head up to the top of the mountain away from people."

"Why?" Than asked. When Jen didn't answer right away, he said, "Jen? Talk to us."

Jen looked from Than to Therese and then back to Than. "The Maenads are coming."

An ice cold chill ran down Therese's back, and the hair stood up at the nape of her neck. "But…"

"We've got a plan," Jen said. "Follow me!"

Thanatos gripped the saddle horn as Jen led him up the mountain. Why hadn't it ever occurred to him that an oath he broke as a god would come back to haunt him as a mortal? And what kind of plan could possibly save him from death?

He loved the life that he and Therese had built together this past year in Colorado. Because of his family's riches, Than hadn't had to work. So as not to be bored, he had taken a part-time job as a tour guide with a whitewater rafting company during the week. It wasn't anything like Charon's raft; in fact, it was far more exciting. Guiding the tourists along the Animas River had helped bridge the gap between his life as a god and his new mortal one.

And Therese worked on Saturdays at an animal shelter in Durango. Even though she couldn't help people and their animal companions on the same scale as she had been able to as a goddess, her work was still important, and he knew it brought her great satisfaction.

The best part of their life was spending every day and night with their twins. Before the twins could walk, Than and Therese would carry them on their backs as they hiked the trails leading up the mountain from the Melner Cabin where they lived. Therese taught them the names of all the trees, plants, and animals. She showed them how to leave food for the birds, chipmunks, deer, rabbits, and wild horses.

Than and Therese also took the twins and Lynn canoeing and swimming in the summer across the dirt road in Lemon Reservoir. Hermie and Hestie learned to swim before they learned to walk and had constantly amazed Than and Therese with how smart and gifted they were. Before they were six months old, they could recite their alphabet and numbers and identify shapes and colors. At twelve months of age, their vocabulary was already as good as that of most adults.

They'd been a source of great pride and joy, and now all of that could be taken away from Than. When he'd made his decision to become mortal, why hadn't he thought of the Maenads?

He wondered if it was too late to take his immortality back. But if he did, what would happen to Pete? Would he immediately lose his body as his soul returned to Tartarus? Would he pass on to the Elysian Fields and never know Tizzie again?

Therese said something, but Than hadn't heard. She was in front of him on Stormy's back.

"What?" he asked.

She said something again, but he still couldn't make out her words. Then he realized why he couldn't hear her: his heart was thumping loudly in his head.

He looked up at her blankly, noticing how beautiful she looked. Her face was flushed, her red hair danced wildly in the wind, and her green eyes were wide with wonder. When she pointed behind him, he turned. That's when he knew what she'd been trying to say. About ten yards down the trail, a satyr appeared. Even in the diminished light of the setting sun, he could tell a satyr from any other kind of creature.

"Faster!" Thanatos cried.

Their horses scrambled up the mountain. Thanatos was numb to the branches scraping against his arms and thighs. He turned back to see more satyrs, with the Maenads right behind them.

When they reached the summit, Than was shocked to see his brother standing on the highest rock.

"Hip?" Therese asked before looking back at Than.

Than had a sinking feeling in his chest. "What are you doing here?"

"We don't have time to explain," Hip said. "Just get behind me."

"What?" Than was at a loss, and, when he turned back, he saw the Maenads were only inches from reaching him.

"Now!" the voice of Hades rang out, though the god was invisible.

Before Than could react, a Maenad grabbed his arm and flung him to the ground. As Therese's screams echoed over the mountaintop, Than was surrounded. The Maenads bore down on him, pulling him in all directions. He felt the snap of his right elbow and heard the sharp crack of breaking bone. He moaned from the excruciating pain as his head began to spin. Then, suddenly, he was being lifted from the mob. He blinked several times when he heard more screams echoing all around. They were the screams of his brother.

He fought the darkness that was descending over him and opened his eyes. He found himself hovering above the mountain in his father's chariot. Hades wore the helm of invisibility. Therese sat on the other side of Than, weeping.

As his senses returned, Than understood what his father had just done: he'd saved one son from the Maenads only to hand over another.

Than looked down to see Jen fighting like a mad woman in the frenzied mob below as she collected the bits of Hip that had been ripped apart by the Maenads and collected them in a golden blanket. Stormy flew above, distracting the drunken women, who tried again and again to grab the flying horse by his hooves to pull him down into their madness. As the Maenads jumped and reached, without success, for Stormy, Than noticed something horrifying on the ground at their feet. It was the maimed body of Sugar. The mare had been killed and partially eaten by Dionysus's tribe.

Pete, now the god of death, appeared among the carnage, making himself visible to Than. He had come for the souls of Hip and Sugar. Looking exactly as he had appeared the day of his death, with his eyes in their sockets and with no sign that his body had ever been dead, Pete gave Than a solemn nod just before he disappeared.

Than put an arm around Therese. He knew what she was thinking. She was thinking this was all her fault. If she'd successfully completed the challenges his father had given her, Than wouldn't have had to break his oath to make her a goddess. But this wasn't her fault, and he needed her to know that. This was *his* fault. When he'd made the trade with Pete, he should have remembered the Maenads. And now his brother had been tortured in his place and a beautiful animal had lost its life, all because of Than.

Tears filled his eyes.

Hades drove the chariot down toward Jen and helped her board with the golden blanket holding Hypnos's remains. Then the chariot—every one of its passengers solemn, silent, and with eyes full of tears—sped across the evening sky and descended through the nearest chasm to the Underworld.

CHAPTER THREE

New Places

Jen had never disintegrated for such a long period of time. Sure, she'd taken over Hip's duties for a few hours here and there, but never had she gone an entire day. While she lay in the asphodel and visited the dreams of millions of sleeping mortals—including the sweet dreams of Hermie and Hestie—she also stood before Scylla inside a dark cave and was having trouble hearing what the monster had to say.

Scylla's six long necks stretched up to the high ceiling of the cave where six round gruesome heads, cut in half by three rows of teeth, peered down at her. Only the four center heads possessed eyes—one each. And they were glaring down at Jen.

Raising her enormous pincers, Scylla said, "I need the potion."

"I thought we swore on the River Styx," Jen insisted. "Why do you need to see it first? Children are suffering right now, every day. We need to do this thing!"

Scylla took an intimidating step toward Jen on her twelve tentacle-like legs. "Oh, I believe you when you say you *intend* to get it. But I'm not certain you're capable of coming through for me."

Jen lifted her chin. "You don't think I can do it."

"I'm not going to anger my parents by forming an alliance with you unless I know it's going to be worth it. Get me the potion first. Then I'll destroy those fishing boats and help you save the children."

Great. Jen had been hoping they would do this in the reverse order. Children were *dying*. "Fine."

Jen mounted Stormy and left Scylla's cave, heading for Circe's island. She knew she should wait for Hip to help her, but every day that passed meant more pain, suffering, and death for the fishing children. It had occurred to her to ask for help from Meg or Tizzie—they probably knew something about Circe's lair—but she was afraid they'd make fun of her plan or, worse, try to talk her out of it. No, if she wanted to save Scylla *and* the children, she'd have to do this on her own.

Her powers of disintegration would, at least, give her an advantage as she tried to maneuver around booby traps, right? Sweat broke out on her forehead and palms as she rode Stormy across the Ionian Sea for the witch's lair.

As she and Stormy descended toward the island, Jen wondered if she ought to ask Hermes for help. Of all the gods outside of the Underworld, he'd always been the kindest to her, and he was probably the least likely to make fun of her for working with a monster. Aphrodite had been kind, too, but the goddess of love was loyal to that Pa*shit*ea, Hip's ex and someone Jen would never trust—ever.

Hermes had been a friend to Jen, but what if he told the other gods what she was up to and they all ganged up on her? No one cared as much as she did about the dozens of small children who were suffering every day at the hands of those cruel fishing companies. Besides, she was a goddess now. Nothing could hurt her anymore, right?

"Oh, Stormy," she whispered. "Tell me I'm doing the right thing."

He whinnied a "Don't ask *me*," which wasn't helpful. At all.

Hip sat in Tartarus on a rock ledge wishing he could convince Jen to wait the week or two his body needed to heal. But he knew his wishful thinking was futile; she would go to Circe's lair without him.

His thoughts were interrupted by the arrival of Than and Therese and their kids.

"Hey, bro," Hip said. "What are you guys doing here?"

"We came to thank you," Therese said.

"I heard your prayers," he said. "Enough, already."

Than's right arm was in a cast and sling. "We wanted to thank you in person."

"Besides, you haven't been able to interact with Hermie and Hestie while they're awake," Therese added. "But now that you're…" Therese dropped off awkwardly.

"Awww. That's the best thank you *ever*." Hip mussed up the boy's dark curls, the same shade as his father's, and when that got him a smile, he did the same to the girl's red ones.

Hestie, the girl, sucked on her index finger and seemed to be thinking of something.

Hermie, the boy, looked around the caverns, taking everything in, until he settled his eyes on Hip and asked, "Why can I see through you?"

Hestie pulled her finger from her mouth. "It's because he has no body, you idiot."

"Language," Therese said, the same way Mrs. Holt—now Mrs. Stern—had said to Jen countless times. "We don't call people idiots."

"But you called that man on TV one, Mommy," Hestie argued.

"Busted," Hip teased.

"That was different," Therese said. "He couldn't hear me, and he wasn't my brother."

"And unlike Hermie, he really was an idiot," Than added.

Therese gave Than a disapproving look.

"Why didn't you bring Clifford?" Hip asked Therese.

"He wants to come when Cubie and Galin are here," Therese explained.

Her dog, Clifford, granted immortality as a gift from Artemis, missed Hecate's familiars. Cubie the Doberman and Galin the polecat had been his constant companions when they had all lived together in the Underworld. But during the spring and summer, Cubie and Galin accompanied Hecate and Persephone to Mount Olympus for six months before returning home to Hades. They wouldn't be home for another few weeks.

"That makes sense." Hip turned back to the twins. "Hey, guys. Come, here and let your Uncle Hip get a good look at you."

The twins took a step closer to him.

"You both look a little different from the projections I see in the Dreamworld."

"What does that mean?" Hestie put her finger in her mouth.

Hip glanced up at Than. "You haven't explained projections to them, bro'? What kind of father are you?"

"They're only a year old," Therese interrupted. "We have lots to teach them, believe me."

"Well, consider this another lesson from your Uncle Hip, got it?" Hip winked at Hestie. "When you sleep, you sometimes project yourself in a way that looks different from the way you look outside of the Dreamworld."

"Like when I'm bigger and stronger in my dreams?" Hermie asked.

"Exactly," Hip said with a nod.

"But then we wake up, and we're our *real* self," Hestie added.

Hip frowned. "The Dreamworld isn't any less real. It's just temporary and filled with figments."

"Dreams are real?" Hermie looked up at his father.

"In a manner of speaking," Than said.

Therese patted Hestie's shoulder. "Maybe this is a lesson for another day."

Hestie pulled on her mother's arm. "We get it, Mommy. We're smart, remember?"

Therese kissed the top of her daughter's head. "I remember."

"I've already taught them about figments, haven't I, kids?" Hip reached out and touched the tip of each of their noses.

The twins nodded.

"They're funny looking," Hestie said with a laugh.

"Uncle Hip told us what to say to make them change," Hermie pointed out. "We say, 'Figment, I command you to show yourself!'"

With his good arm, Than patted his son's curls. "That's right, Hermie. Good job."

"What's this?" Tizzie's voice rang out from across the cavernous room.

"Tizzie?" Therese asked with surprise.

In another instant Tizzie was standing beside Hip, smiling down at the twins. "No one told me you were coming for a visit! I'm so happy to see you!"

"Do you remember your Aunt Tizzie?" Than asked the kids.

Before they could answer, Tizzie kissed the two children all over their faces. "I haven't seen you since before you could walk!" Tizzie's serpentine hair briefly became animated snakes that hissed, causing Hermie to scream.

Tizzie's hair settled down. "Sorry about that!"

Hestie pulled her finger from her mouth. "I think I remember you. I'm not sure."

"Grampa Hades told us about her, remember, Hestie?" Hermie said. "But he didn't tell us about her snake hair."

Hestie nodded.

"Grampa Hades?" Hip laughed. "I can't believe my ears."

"Oh, hush," Tizzie said. "You don't have any ears."

"Good one." Hip sneered at his sister.

"Just kidding," Tizzie said. "Don't be so sensitive."

"I wish I could have seen Hades interacting with you little ones," Hip said to the kids. Was Hades gentle with the twins, or distant? Ever since they'd found out that Zeus had deceived them all by disguising himself as Hades and fathering Melinoe—which he then tried to cover up by attempting to destroy her in the womb—Hip's parents had been tender toward one another and nicer to others in general. "What did ol' Grampa Hades say?"

"He took us to see his dog," Hermie said.

"We got to ride on his back," Hestie added.

"But only after we fed him cake, right kids?" Than reminded them.

"Right," Hestie said.

"Never approach Cerberus without cake," Meg said as she and Alecto appeared on either side of Tizzie.

As the gods of the Underworld visited with Than's family, Hip was bothered by a tinge of jealousy. Zeus had agreed to the demands of the Athena Alliance for equality between the male and female deities under the condition that no more gods would be produced. All deities were rendered sterile by Hera. When they were married, Jen and Hip had both come to terms with that. Jen had even said she never wanted any kids, probably because of what her father had put her through. But now, as Hip watched Than with his little ones, he wished he, too, could be a father one day.

Jen dismounted Stormy. "Stay here in the woods where it's safe."

Stormy cocked his head to the side.

"I'll be fine. But if I'm not back in an hour, go get help."

She made her way through the thick forest up the hill. When she reached the summit, she spotted Circe's house down in the clearing below. It wasn't at all what she'd been expecting. It looked more like a modern building than a witch's lair—all stone and glass and sharp angles. It sparkled in the early morning sun.

Jen continued across the summit and started her trek down the other side of the hill, toward the house. Three wolves lying near the stoop sat up on their haunches and sniffed in her direction. Three more joined them from behind the house, and then all six began to pace nervously near the front door. Normally, a pack of wolves would frighten her, but she was a goddess now.

When she neared the front yard, the wolves stared at her.

"Hey, there, boys," she said gently.

Upon closer inspection, they all seemed gaunt, as though they hadn't eaten in days.

"You boys look like you could use a good meal."

A loud squeal made her jump. The wolves turned toward the house and began to bark.

Was someone trapped inside?

Slowly, she continued toward the front door. When she was about ten yards away, two mountain lions sprang from out of nowhere and bounded toward her. She turned to run, and then remembered her goddess strength. She could take them. Standing her ground, she waited for them to pounce.

Instead, they stopped in front of her and slinked their backs against her legs like common house cats.

Jen let out the breath she'd been holding and continued toward the front door.

Before she turned the knob, she heard another squeal from inside. Two of the wolves scratched against the wooden door, wanting to be let in. They were more concerned with whatever was squealing than they were with her.

Remembering what Hip had said about booby traps, Jen opened the door and stood back as the wolves rushed inside. What happened next made her stomach turn. The wolves knocked over a unit of shelving, and all of the glass containers crashed onto the white stone floor. Preserved animal parts and foul-smelling formaldehyde spilled everywhere. Jen gagged when the wolves stepped over the broken glass to eat the animal parts—frog legs, the snouts of pigs, whole rats, and the tails and tongues of who-knew-what. As Jen looked over the sight, her heart sank in her chest. Had Circe's potions been among those broken bottles?

Another loud squeal echoed throughout the room, and then its source became apparent as a pig scurried past the wolves, brushed by Jen's leg, and scrambled out the front door. Before it had gotten very far, the two mountain lions attacked it in the yard and devoured it.

Jen turned away, disgusted.

Across the room, a large black cauldron sat on the hearth. Heaps of ash lay around it along the grate. To the side of the hearth, a long tapestry hung on the wall and draped in piles on the floor. The silken fabric depicted scenes like Jen had found in storybooks—flying horses, girls in pretty dresses, men carrying swords into battle, and chariots driven by gods. Beyond the tapestry, along the adjacent wall, was another unit of shelves covered with bottles and jars.

"Those must be her potions," Jen whispered to herself.

Carefully, she stepped across the slippery stone floor, dodging the dogs and the broken glass. If she were more confident, she could attempt to fly, but she just wasn't there yet. When she reached the shelving unit, she began stuffing her bag with the dozen or so bottles, but before she had collected them all, the floor dropped below her, and a powerful force sucked her down.

She clawed at anything to break her fall. Her efforts were futile.

She landed on her bottom on hard dirt and gravel. The air was warm, moist, and suffocating. With her goddess vision, she looked around in the darkness for a way out. The trap door twenty feet above her had shut closed. She wondered if she could manage to fly up and push it open. If not, could she climb up there? She studied the earthen walls and gravel floor. Then she froze. Something in the corner across from her moved.

C H A P T E R   F O U R

Missing

Hip laughed as his niece and nephew attempted to fist-bump his transparent fist. "Maybe we'll try this again when I'm in better form." But he supposed that could never be possible, since he would only put them straight to sleep. He was glad no one bothered to point that out, especially since Tizzie had just made fun of him for not having ears.

"Where are you headed now?" Meg asked Than and Therese.

"Therese wants to show the kids her favorite bat cave," Than said.

"NUH-ner-NUh-ner-NUh-ner-NUH-ner, BATMAN!" Hip sang.

The kids looked back at him blankly.

"What?" he asked. "You guys haven't heard of Batman?" He turned to Than. "Seriously, what kind of parents are you?"

Therese rolled her eyes. "We'll see you later, Hip."

"Mind if I come with?" Tizzie asked.

Hermie shrugged. "I'm okay with it, as long as your hair stays like *that*."

The others laughed.

"Now don't be rude," Meg warned Hermie, with a hint of red in her eyes.

Hermie grabbed his mother's hand.

"I promise to keep my hair under better control," Tizzie said to Hermie with a smile.

"Well, I need to get back to work," Alecto said. "Those evildoers won't punish *themselves.*"

"And I have some avenging to do in the Middle East." Meg kissed each of the twins on the cheek. "I hope to see you both again soon."

Before the two Furies departed, Hades appeared.

"Grampa Hades!" Hestie said gleefully.

But Hades had no tenderness for her. He looked directly at Hip and said, "Stormy just arrived at the stables without Jen."

"What?" Therese cried. "Where is she?"

Hades turned to her. "Apparently, she's gone to Circe's island." Then he turned to Hip. "Did you know about this?"

"She may have mentioned something to me." Hip told them about the fishing companies in Ghana, how they were abusing children, and Jen's deal with Scylla. "I told her to wait."

"This is not the best timing, Hypnos," Hades grumbled. "I just received word from Hermes about another attack on Gaia."

"Oh, great," Meg complained.

"Attack on Gaia? Where?" Than asked.

Hip realized Than hadn't been kept in the loop, now that he was mortal.

"A volcano in Russia," Hades said. "And that's not the worst of it."

"Let me guess." Alecto put her hands on her hips. "Another Giant escaped."

Therese's mouth dropped open. "What?"

Hades nodded.

Than put an arm around Therese's waist. "Sounds like there's a lot we don't know, but, right now, we need to focus on Jen. Stormy wouldn't just abandon her. Something must have happened."

"Agreed," Hip said. "Someone needs to go look for her."

Just then, Hecate appeared. "Persephone's worried sick. She said she's already lost one son and can't abide losing another." Hecate glanced at Thanatos.

"She hasn't exactly *lost* me," Than mumbled.

"What's going on that I've been called to the duties of Sleep?" Hecate asked Hip.

"Oh, no," Hip moaned.

Hades filled her in—both on what had happened with the Maenads and Jen's deal with Scylla.

"She must be trapped or badly injured," Hip said. "Those are the only reasons she'd lose her power of disintegration."

"I wish there was something we could do to help," Therese said.

"Should Alecto and I search the island?" Meg asked Hades.

"I can help, too," Tizzie offered.

"Go," Hades said. "And better take Hecate. She knows more about dark magic than anyone."

"I'm happy to serve," Hecate said.

Therese put a hand on Hecate's shoulder. "It's so good to see you again. Please be careful."

Hecate gave Therese a smile before she and the Furies disappeared.

Hip met his father's gaze. "I tried to talk Jen out of this."

"She's doing her job," Hades said. "She's got guts, initiative."

"I've never felt so helpless," Than muttered.

"Tell me about it," Hip said.

Hades tugged at his beard. "We'll find her. Meanwhile, I'll ask Apollo if there's anything he can do to speed your body's recovery along."

Hip was surprised when Hades patted each of the twins on their heads. "You two be good and mind your parents. You have an important destiny awaiting you."

Hestie pulled her finger from her mouth. "We do?"

"We haven't talked to them about that yet," Than said to Hades.

"What destiny?" Hermie asked.

"Come on," Therese said, taking each of their hands. "Let's go look at the bats."

Once Than had left with his family and he was alone with his father, Hip said, "Please do everything you can to find her."

Hades lifted his hand, as though about to clap it onto Hip's shoulder, and then must have thought better of it. "You have my word."

Jen pressed her back against the earthy wall of her prison. "Who's there?"

A black cloak twirled around, and the hood dropped, revealing the face of…Ariadne?

"Jen? Is that you?" Ariadne asked. "Oh, thank the gods!"

"What are you doing down here?" Jen asked.

Ariadne brushed her dark bangs from her green eyes. "I came here for Circe's potions."

"Really? Why?"

"Hoping to help Asterion." The Minotaur's sister lifted her palms in the air. "He doesn't know I came. I told him I needed a break from the labyrinth and was going to spend time with Dionysus for a while. That's why no one's come looking for me. No one realizes I've been missing."

"Oh, my gosh."

"I was wondering how long it would be before I ever saw another person again."

"How long have you been down here?"

"I'm not sure. Maybe five or six days."

"You poor thing."

"It's made me appreciate the labyrinth. At least there, I can walk around and go out for fresh air."

"And play night Frisbee."

"Oh, how I miss that. We haven't played in ages."

"I still suck at flying."

"It's all in your head, Jen. Asterion was the same way."

"Really? So it's not just me?"

"No, absolutely not. There have been many people who began as mortals who needed time to adjust. It's perfectly normal."

"That's a relief."

"Asterion and I were both born as mortals. You know his story, right?"

Jen shook her head.

"Poseidon sent my father a snow-white bull to be sacrificed, but when my father didn't do what he was supposed to, Poseidon made my poor mother fall in love with the bull. Our mother, Pasiphae, is a goddess, and my father was King Minos—he's now one of the judges for Hades, but he was a mortal king before that."

"Really?"

"In fact, Circe is my mother's sister," Ariadne added. "Though they haven't spoken in decades. Once Circe went dark, no one wanted anything to do with her."

"Wow. I didn't know that."

"Anyway, my problem wasn't flying. I was afraid no one would love me. I even betrayed my own brother because of it. I was really pathetic, actually."

"Well, thank you for that, but, as happy as I am to keep you company, I have no idea how to get us out of here. Have you tried anything?"

Ariadne crossed her arms and sighed. "Oh, yes. There's no way to open that trap door above us, and there's no other way out. There's also a protective barrier that makes it impossible for me to reach anyone through prayer."

"That's why I can't disintegrate," Jen mumbled.

"Huh?"

"I had to take over the duties of Sleep for Hip."

"Why? Is he alright?"

Jen explained about the Maenads. She told her about Sugar, too, recalling the look on Bobby's face when she'd given him the news.

"Oh, those horrible Maenads. How Dionysus can stand to be in their company every night is beyond me."

Jen heard a noise, like a drip, coming from somewhere behind Ariadne. "What's that sound?"

Ariadne listened. "Oh, you mean this. It's water. It's just a little bit running in, but it's kept me feeling clean and refreshed all this time, thank goodness."

This gave Jen an idea. She crossed the pit to inspect the wall. The water seeped in at a point just above their heads. "This is sea water. We must be below sea level in here."

"I'm sure we are. Why?"

"We can dig our way out!"

"Knowing Circe, it won't be that easy," Ariadne warned.

"But we have to try, don't we?"

"I don't have any better ideas," Ariadne admitted.

Jen touched the damp part of the wall and used her fingers to pull away at the rock and earth. With her goddess strength, she managed to pry a melon-sized chunk, which fell to the ground at her feet. Sea water streamed into the pit, and, luckily, the flow wasn't as strong as she had anticipated.

"Help me," Jen said, as she pried more earth and rock with her bare hands.

Soon, she and Ariadne had created a tunnel about three-feet in diameter and five feet long, through which Jen could see a large cavern. Sea water flooded through in a stream about a foot deep, and it was coming from a pool on the other side.

Jen hoisted herself into the wet tunnel. "Come on."

Ariadne grabbed her boot. "Be careful. Like I said, it can't be this easy."

Jen crawled through the five-foot long tunnel and landed in a pool of rushing water in the much larger cavern. At an angle to the current, she swam to the rocky bank on the other side. The cavern was as black as pitch, and Jen was still getting used to being able to see in the dark. As she climbed onto the bank, she realized she'd been holding her breath in the water, even though she no longer had to as a goddess. She wondered how long it would take her to get used to all of her new powers. Hip hated the water, so they rarely spent time in it.

She turned back to see Ariadne following. Jen held out her hand, intending to help the other goddess to her feet, but Ariadne flew from the pool and landed on the bank beside Jen.

Jen shook her head. Why hadn't she tried to fly, too? Oh, yeah. Because she couldn't.

"Maybe we can god travel from here," Ariadne said. She balled her fists and sighed. "No. I guess not. Circe's enchantments must reach out here, too."

"Let's follow the water upstream," Jen said. "It should lead us to the sea."

They followed on foot for as long as they could. After a half mile of trekking along the ever-narrowing cave, the opening became too small. If they were to continue, they'd have to swim.

Jen was not afraid of the water. She was a strong swimmer. But she was afraid of whatever sea life might be in there. Even though she was a goddess, her disgust for all things slimy—whether they could harm her or not—had not gone away.

"I guess we should swim for it," she said to Ariadne.

Ariadne gave her a reluctant nod. "Just be vigilant."

Jen dived into the dark cold water, wishing Ariadne would take the lead. Jen paused, looking all around her for signs of creatures as she adjusted to the practice of breathing underwater. When Ariadne waited for her to go first, Jen moved on.

The first thing she noticed was that the water had become much deeper. She wondered if the way out was down. Using the breaststroke, she swam toward the bottom, to investigate, when suddenly something long, black, and slimy grabbed her by the leg.

CHAPTER FIVE

Enemies and Allies

Hip had only been in Tartarus for two days, and he was already impatient to leave. He supposed he wouldn't have minded the staycation if Jen hadn't gone missing. He couldn't stop worrying about her and all the horrible situations she might be in right now, and there was nothing he could do to help her.

Had he made a mistake when he'd given her his immortality?

No. Absolutely not. She would have died in Circe's battlefield after Echidna had bashed her against the rock cave. He'd had no choice but to save Jen. He loved her more than he'd ever loved anyone. And that was saying something, because, boy, had he loved a lot of women. He never loved them for long, and he never loved them deeply. Pasithea had been the only person he'd come close to caring about, and even that hadn't been the same.

Jen was such a sweetheart. *His* sweetheart. Oh, gods, how he wished he had his body back so he could go and look for her.

He prayed to the Furies again. They'd been gone for hours.

Any sign of her?

No. Meg replied. *There's nothing here but a mess.*

We've searched every room, every cupboard, every closet, Alecto added.

We even discovered traps and pits and found no sign of her, Tizzie said.

But this broken glass and overturned furniture worries me, Meg said.

The fact that they'd found signs of a struggle had alarmed him, too. Where could Jen be?

Check with Scylla, he said. *Maybe the crab is holding Jen prisoner.*

Will do, Tizzie replied.

Jen struggled and kicked against the black slimy thing that was pulling her down into the cold, dark water. The thing merely tightened its grip.

Think! She had to stop panicking and think!

She stopped kicking and pulling and really looked at the thing. Oh, dear gods, it was an enormous black octopus.

Jen froze, in total shock.

In the next moment, Ariadne was beside her with her sword conjured. The goddess severed the tentacle and pulled Jen free, but before they could god travel away, they were each grabbed by another tentacle, and this time, they were dragged through the water at an incredibly high speed.

Jen tried to keep her eyes open, even though she was terrified. They were still inside a system of caverns and tunnels. She felt like she was on the most horrifying water ride in the world. At least five whole minutes of terror went by before she and Ariadne were flung into the air inside another large cave.

Ariadne flew up and helped to brace Jen's fall.

"Thanks," Jen said, panting.

Jen caught her balance and her breath as she looked around. She recognized where she was right away. This was Scylla's cave! The opening to the Messina Straight stretched wide across the pool from the opposite bank.

"Scylla?" Jen called out.

Ariadne turned to her with furrowed brows. "What are you doing? Don't you want to get out of here? Let's go?"

"You go," Jen said. "This is actually where I was headed. Scylla and I have a deal."

"Oh, you do, do you?" came a voice from the other side of the cavern.

Jen turned to see Keto lift herself from the pool onto the bank on the other side of the cave. Her silver, mermaid tail flicked off water, like a wet dog, before settling down on the rock.

"What kind of deal?" Keto asked.

Ariadne prayed, *Jen, we need to go now!* And then she disappeared.

"Where's Scylla?" Jen asked Keto. "She's expecting me."

"You didn't answer my question."

Jen crossed her arms. "It's none of your business."

Keto arched a brow.

This dame was scary. Jen wondered if she should follow Ariadne and come back later, when Keto wasn't around. As she was just about to leave, however, Scylla emerged from the water and towered over her.

"Did you get it?" she asked Jen.

"I think so." Jen patted the bag strapped across her chest.

"Get what?" Keto asked.

Scylla turned in surprise at the sound of her mother's voice. "Mother? What are you doing here?"

"Looking for you. But apparently, I'm not the only one." The mermaid dipped into the water and swam to the bank beside Jen.

"Well, here I am. What do you want?" Scylla demanded.

"Go ahead and finish your business. I'll wait."

Scylla glanced at Jen and then back at her mother. "*She* can wait. Now tell me why you came."

"I'd rather not say in mixed company," Keto said in an icy voice. "Now do as I say and finish your business so we can talk."

Jen didn't like how close Keto had come to her. "I'll come back when you're not busy," Jen said to Scylla.

"You'll do no such thing," Keto said. Then she whistled.

From the depths of the water, the black octopus arose and wrapped another tentacle around Jen. This time, it had her by the waist and squeezed so hard that she could barely breathe.

"I'm tired of not being treated with respect anymore," Keto said. "I was once the queen of these waters. It's time others were reminded of that."

At that moment, something enormous rushed in from the opening to the Messina Straight. Jen quickly realized it wasn't another monster but a group of goddesses—Hecate and the Furies, along with their familiars. Tizzie and Meg's hair was in full snake form, and blood dripped from their eyes. Alecto's red hair had become flames as she bound Keto with her familiar—a python as long as the octopus's tentacles. Tizzie had Scylla bound with a golden whip, while her wolf growled at Scylla menacingly. And Meg and Hecate, along with Meg's falcon, charged the octopus, setting Jen free.

"Come on!" Meg cried, grabbing Jen by the hand.

Like a swarm of bats, they all flew from the cave and god traveled directly to the Underworld to Hades's main chamber.

Jen hadn't even had the chance to catch her breath when Hades turned to her and said, "Now tell me about this deal."

She swallowed hard and then told him about the fishing companies in Ghana, the abused children, her deal with Scylla, and getting trapped in Circe's lair with Ariadne. She told how they had dug their way out but then were taken prisoner by Keto's octopus.

"I understand your motives," Hades said when she had finished. "What I don't understand is why you would go to Scylla for help instead of turning to your true allies."

"You mean Poseidon?" Jen asked. She'd thought about asking him but didn't feel she knew him well enough. Plus, he scared her even more than Hades did.

"No," Tizzie said. "He means us."

"We could have helped you," Alecto said.

"And we still can," Meg pointed out.

"You don't need Scylla," Hecate said.

Hades turned to the Furies. "You've been detained from your duties long enough."

They each nodded and disappeared.

Hades turned to Hecate. "Give my love to Persephone, will you?"

"As always," she said before she, too, vanished.

Hades turned now to Jen. "All of this could have been prevented had you come to me first."

"This was about more than the children of Ghana," she said, trying hard to stand up for herself. "This was also about Scylla. She was a victim, too. Keto tried to kill her and has been cruel to her."

"That's what monsters do," Hades said.

Jen took a deep breath, trying to keep from backing down. She was a goddess now, and she had to act like one. "Scylla doesn't want to be a monster. Everyone ought to have a choice."

"But we *don't*," Hades said with a tinge of anger in his voice. "We *don't* have a choice. We have a *destiny*."

"Then we should do all we can to shape our destinies," Jen said. "I get that there are limits to what we can control, but we should try to control what we can, to be the captains of our own ships."

That's what her mother used to always tell her. She would say, "Jen, you need to be the captain of your own ship, baby doll."

When Hades narrowed his eyes at her but said nothing, she continued, "When I became the goddess of abused children and was able to turn my difficult past into a way of helping others, I became a new person—a liberated person. If Scylla can save these children, maybe she can save herself, too."

Hades scratched his chin and looked down his nose at her. "I see now why you and Therese are friends."

Jen wasn't sure how to take that.

Hip jumped up from his rock in Tartarus when Jen suddenly appeared. "I've been worried sick."

"I know," she said. "I'm sorry, but…"

"It's okay." He tried to hold her, but his transparent arms were useless. "Gods, I can't wait to get my body back."

"You're not mad?"

He gave her a smile. "Let's just say a little birdie reminded me that you're just doing your job."

She kissed the air in front of his face and laughed. "I don't know how Tizzie did it for so long."

"Did what?"

"Kissed my brother, Pete, while he was down here in Tartarus without his body. It's impossible."

Hip shook his head. "Ye of little faith."

He carefully cupped her face with his airy hands and pressed his transparent lips to hers, where he whispered, "Use your imagination."

Her soft moan titillated him in ways he didn't think possible for a bodiless soul.

When Hip smiled down at her, she asked, "Any idea how much longer?"

"Apollo said three more days." He sat back down on his rock ledge.

She sat beside him. "Geez. They'll be the longest of my life."

"Are you Sleep again?" he asked.

She nodded. "And that reminds me…When you're running around in the Dreamworld, are you still kissing other girls?"

Hip lifted his airy chin. "Well, of course. It's my job."

"Oh, okay. Then you don't mind if I make out with the Hemsworth boys?"

"You mean the actors?"

"Yeah. The really hot ones. One played Thor, the other played Gale…"

"Okay, okay," he said, not happy with where this was going. "I guess we could send figments to do our dirty work."

"My point exactly."

"I really did meet my match the day I met you, didn't I?" he said without inflection.

"You bet your bottom drachma. Now promise me you'll stop making out in the Dreamworld."

Hip had to admit that ever since he'd fallen in love with Jen, the make out sessions had lost a lot of their appeal. In fact, playing in the Dreamworld had even become tiresome to him. He'd rather be with Jen. "Let's make a deal."

She looked at him sideways. "I'm listening."

"I promise to stop making out in the Dreamworld, if you promise to think about having a child together."

Jen's brows disappeared beneath her blonde fringe. "But that's impossible. Zeus decreed…"

"I know, I know. But if I could get him to change his mind, would you be open to it?"

Jen bit her bottom lip. He wanted badly to bite it too.

"I'll think about it," she said. "Okay?"

"That's all I'm asking," he said.

"So we have a deal?"

"We have a deal. You can stop kissing what's-his-face."

She smiled. "Oh, darn. How did you know I was still making out?"

He rolled his transparent eyes and laughed. He knew she was kidding—at least, he hoped she was.

C H A P T E R   S I X

The Best Laid Plans

Jen sat on a stool at the kitchen bar of the Melner Cabin across from Therese. Clifford lay curled in a ball near her feet.

"If Hip is still in Tartarus, why aren't you Sleep?" Therese asked from the kitchen sink, where she was washing the last of her breakfast dishes.

"I got Hecate to take over for me—just for a little while."

"So why come for a visit now, when you're so busy?"

"You're still my best friend," Jen said. "And I need your advice."

When Hades had asked Jen why she had gone to Scylla instead of to her real allies, what Jen had said about Scylla needing to be a hero was true, but there was another reason. Jen felt as though she'd been depending on her Underworld family for almost a year now, and she wanted to prove to them that she could accomplish things without them. She didn't mind getting help from Scylla, or any other god outside of the Underworld; however, she needed to show Hip and his family that she could do it without *them*.

Therese dried her hands and turned from the window, where her two favorite redbirds were singing their morning song. "This sounds serious."

A very short Batman suddenly appeared from the living room beside Jen. He stopped, crossed his arms, and, in a low guttural breath, said, "To the bat cave, Robin. There's not a moment to lose."

An even shorter Robin, in pig tails, no less, darted around the corner and headed down the basement stairs. "I'm on it, Batman!"

Clifford pricked up his ears.

Jen stifled a giggle. "Can they handle the stairs? Oh, I guess so."

Batman practically flew after his sister, and Clifford followed, leaving Jen alone with Therese.

"My gosh, they're fast," Jen said. "They act more like they're *five*, not *one*. I can't believe it."

"They blow my mind."

"What do your aunt and uncle think?"

"So far, we've been able to keep them in the dark."

"That won't last. It can't. You have to tell them."

Therese sighed. "I'm thinking about it."

Jen leaned across the counter toward Therese. "What's holding you back?"

"I just want my kids to live normal human lives for as long as possible, you know?"

"What's so great about normal?" Jen crinkled her nose. "Why not let them be themselves?"

"I want them to fit in. I'm worried about how others will treat them. Right now, they have only each other, but what about when they start school? How will their teachers and classmates treat them when they see how different my babies are?"

"How different *are* they?"

"They're fast, strong, smart, and growing bigger much faster than the average person."

"Do they have any special powers other than speed, strength, and smarts?" Jen asked.

"What do you mean? Isn't that enough?"

"You know. Like how Percy Jackson could manipulate water. Anything like that?"

Therese laughed. "This is real life, Jen. I don't think they're going to have any special powers."

"Why not?"

"Don't you think I've read up on this? Most of the demigods throughout history have been kings, queens, warriors, and princesses. They may have fought monsters, but they didn't manipulate water."

"Really? No superpowers? That's disappointing."

"Well, they weren't without special talents. Orpheus could sing so beautifully that he persuaded the gods to give him back his dead wife."

"See. That's something. Can your kids sing?"

Therese laughed. "I mean, they can carry a tune, but their voices aren't show-stopping or anything."

"Maybe something will develop—something special."

"Hmm. Maybe. More tea?"

"Sure," Jen said. She'd missed simple things, like sweet, iced tea, and like riding the horses in the pastures in the evenings as the sun slowly set behind the mountains. She missed grooming and even spreading hay, though she didn't miss cleaning. While working in the Dreamworld, she managed to simulate some of these experiences from her old life, but it wasn't the same, no matter how often Hip insisted that they were as real as what happened in the Upperworld.

As Therese refilled her glass, Jen asked, "So, what time does Than get home from work?"

"He'll be here sometime after lunch. Will you still be here?"

Jen looked down her nose at her friend. "What do you think?"

Therese blushed. "Yeah, probably not."

Jen sipped her tea, and after a few minutes of awkward silence, asked, "Do you miss it?"

"Every single day." Tears welled in Therese's eyes.

"I'm sorry. *Of course,* you miss it."

Therese shook her head. "No. It's okay." She wiped her eyes with the back of her hand. "So, tell me what's going on."

"I worked out this deal, you know, to save those slave children in Ghana, but I haven't been able to figure out how I'm actually gonna rescue them." Then she quickly added, "I know I could ask Hip or his father or sisters, but I really want to show them that I can do this without them."

"Isn't Scylla helping?"

"She's accosting the boats for me, yeah. But how do we get the kids home to their families? I'll be able to disintegrate, but how will I get them home? I can't even fly." Jen felt her cheeks flush with embarrassment at the admission.

"You'll get the hang of it. Just think of it as swimming in air."

Therese had told her that before. It hadn't worked so well for Jen. Air felt nothing like water.

"Could you borrow Hades's chariot?" Therese asked.

"Not enough room. There's like forty or fifty kids."

Therese sucked on her lower lip, and, for a moment, she looked just like Hestie. "You know who you should ask to help you? Hera."

Jen flinched. "Are you crazy? That woman scares me."

"Yeah. She can be pretty scary."

"Wasn't she your enemy?"

Therese leaned her elbows on the kitchen counter, squaring herself to Jen. "There's something you need to understand about the gods. Very few of them are actually your friends. You can always count on the Underworld gods to be there for you. But the Olympians, except for maybe Hermes, will sometimes be your allies and sometimes be your enemies, depending on the situation. You can't take it personally. It's just the way it is."

"And you think Hera will help me with this?" Jen asked.

"Her duty is to help and protect families," Therese replied. "So, yes. I think she'd have an interest in this."

"Didn't she throw her own son from Mount Olympus?" Jen asked, confused.

"You mean Hephaestus?"

Jen nodded.

"It's rumored that she thought someone had switched him with a monster after birth, because he wasn't perfect, like the other gods."

Jen wasn't sure she believed that, but she didn't have any better ideas. "What do I say to her? How do I approach her?"

Therese smiled. "She loves gifts. And Hera is a sucker for anything made of peacock feathers."

"Oh, like that fan you made her years ago."

"Exactly."

Jen wondered what *she* could give Hera.

"I saw a pretty bag in Durango last weekend," Therese said. "It was trimmed with peacock feathers. It would be perfect."

Jen shook her head. "It's been a long time since I've been shopping in Durango."

Therese giggled. "Might be worth it. Should we go together?"

"What about the twins?" Jen asked.

"We could take them along. Unless you want me to ask Carol to watch them?"

"No. Let's take them. But let's make this quick, okay? The kids are used to god-travel, right? Isn't that how you got them to the Underworld?"

"Yeah. Aphrodite gave me a new traveling robe. It comes in handy when I'm running late."

Jen laughed. "I bet it does. Well, come on then. Let's get this show on the road!"

Hip walked around the corner of his stone wall in Tartarus to see Tizzie at work. She knelt on the chest of a terrified soul. Her snake hair hissed. Blood dripped from her eyes. She was both beautiful and gruesome. Hip admired the way she threw herself into her duties, completely and enthusiastically, but he shuddered, too. He preferred his style of play in the Dreamworld. And even the nightmares, he knew, would come to an end, and a new day would dawn. With that new day, there was always hope.

But not so in Tartarus. While all souls were able to purge themselves of their crimes and pass on to the Fields of Elysium—thanks to the work of Therese on behalf of Melinoe and Tiresias—for whatever reason, many stayed behind. Sisyphus was one of them. Every day, he rolled a giant bolder up a steep hill, and at the end of the day, he watched it roll back down.

Hip returned to the quiet corner where he'd been waiting for his body to heal. Boredom seemed as bad a punishment as pain, but, as much as he'd hoped to entertain himself by watching his sister, he couldn't stomach it. He'd rather sit and wait.

Sometime later, Tizzie came to see him. "It won't be long," she said.

"It may as well be," he said solemnly. "The seconds feel like minutes down here."

"Only when you're dead."

"Haha. Very funny."

"Oh, don't be so sensitive."

"Don't be so rude."

Tizzie put a hand on her hip. "*You* are lecturing *me* about rudeness? That's a first."

He didn't reply. He wasn't in the mood to play.

She sat on the stone ledge beside him. She didn't say anything. He realized after a few moments that she was trying, in her way, to comfort him.

"Hey, Tizzie?" he asked after a while.

"Yes?"

"Do you and Pete ever wish you could have a child?"

"What? Gods, no."

"Why not?" he asked, surprised. "You're always excited around Than's kids."

"And I worry about them constantly," she said. "Having children makes you weak and vulnerable. If I had a kid, and if that kid was ever captured by my enemy? I would do whatever the enemy asked to save my child. He would have me at his mercy. There's no way I want to ever be put in that position. Ever."

She made a good point.

"Besides," she added. "It's impossible, so why think about it?"

Hip shrugged. "I guess you're right."

Jen arrived at the gates of Mount Olympus, unable to recall the words Hip always used to get inside.

"Oh, Geez," she muttered. "This sucks."

The boy from Ghana prayed to her again. His master was beating him with the stick full of thorns because he had complained about how cold the water was.

"Out of my way!" a voice bellowed behind her.

She jumped to the side just in time to avoid getting trampled by three foam-white horses pulling a chariot. Poseidon stood at the reins, his long, sun-bleached hair blowing around his face, as he hollered, "Spring, Summer, Winter, and Fall, open the damn gates of Mount Olympus so that I, Poseidon, lord of the sea, may enter!"

The clouds parted, and, just as the gates slid open, Poseidon and his chariot blew through, like a hurricane. Jen was surprised when she was able to slip in after him.

The courtyard was empty for a few seconds as Poseidon parked his chariot. Jen stood dumbly before the whale fountain, wondering if she should just walk inside. Well, of course she should, shouldn't she? She was a god, just like the others. She was allowed to be here. She turned to climb the rainbow steps, but before she reached the top, Poseidon flew by her again.

"Come on," he said. "We're late."

"Late for what?" she cried breathlessly, but he had already entered without her.

With the peacock purse strapped across her chest and hanging at her hip, she followed him inside to find nearly all the Olympians there. Zeus and Hera both stood in front of their thrones arguing. Athena paced in front of them between her throne and the one belonging to Ares. The god of war wasn't there, because he was still serving at her mom's ranch in Colorado—his punishment for releasing Atlas and putting the entire pantheon in jeopardy.

Hermes looked up and noticed her.

She returned his smile, glad to see a friendly face.

Then Zeus shouted, "Where is Hades? He's late!"

"He must have sent Jen in his place," Persephone said from the double throne she shared with her mother. "Take a seat, dear."

All eyes were on Jen as the court became silent. Then a throne emerged from the marble floor behind her, and Persephone repeated, "Have a seat, dear."

Jen did the only thing she could: she sat.

"Fine then," Zeus muttered. "Let's get down to business. Athena? What do you have to report?"

The goddess of wisdom stood up. "Metis and I questioned Gaia, who swore again on the River Styx that she did not release the Giants on her own."

"Did she describe what happened?" Hermes asked.

Athena's mother, Metis, stepped forward from behind Zeus's throne. "Something hotter than lava struck two different volcanoes in Russia."

"The Giants escaped before Gaia could heal," Athena added.

"What's hotter than lava?" Hestia asked.

"Fire," Hephaestus said. "Fire is hotter than lava."

"And lightning," Poseidon said.

Zeus flew to his feet and trained his glare on his brother. "How dare you!"

"Calm down! I'm not accusing anyone of anything!" Poseidon, equally enraged, barked. "Just stating facts."

Zeus grumbled as he returned to his seat.

Jen wiped the sweat that had broken out on her forehead, wishing she hadn't come.

"The sun and stars are hotter than lava," Apollo pointed out.

"Noted." Then Zeus turned to Poseidon. "Anything suspicious in the seven seas?"

"Nothing unusual," Poseidon said.

Zeus glanced back at Apollo who nodded. Jen understood the exchange. Apollo had confirmed that the sea god had spoken the truth. Poseidon grumbled to show offense had been taken, but Zeus ignored him.

"And how many souls have come to Hades as a result of being killed by these Giants?" Zeus asked.

Everyone turned to Jen. She was overcome with mortification as it dawned on her that they expected her to answer.

Then she remembered that Pete would know. She sent out a prayer to him in desperation.

"Jen?" Aphrodite, who sat to Jen's left, stood up. "Are you not feeling well? You look pale."

Pete hadn't answered her. Jen didn't know what to say.

"Jen, dear?" Persephone asked. "What is it?"

Jen stood up, trying to hide her weak, shaky knees. "Hades didn't send me here. I came on my own for a different reason. I brought Hera a gift." Jen patted the peacock purse.

Hera's face paled, making Jen feel small and dumb.

"As you can see," Zeus said, "this isn't a good time."

"We're discussing something of grave importance," Hera added.

Jen's mission was important, too, but she was too afraid to say so before all of the gods. Her face burned with utter embarrassment as she stood there, trembling, unsure whether she should sit back down on Hades's throne or leave. As tears rushed to her eyes, she bowed her head, not wanting the others to see her face. Just as she had decided she should run from the room, Pete appeared beside her.

He winked at her before turning to Zeus. "My sister said you needed the death toll from the monsters."

"Yes," Zeus said. "Do you have those numbers?"

Jen had never been happier to see her brother.

"I retrieved 231 souls from southern Russia during the initial attack a month ago," Pete said. "Since then, 363 more people have been killed in similar attacks."

"All in Russia?" Artemis asked.

"All but twelve," Pete said. "Last night, I retrieved a dozen souls from Alaska."

"The Giants are moving east?" Apollo asked. "Nothing to the west?"

"No deaths in Europe from the monsters," Pete said. "Not yet, anyway."

"This is important information," Zeus said. "Thank you, Peter Holt. You and your sister may leave."

As Jen turned to follow her brother out, Hera called from across the room. "Leave your gift, and return to me tonight while I sleep."

Jen removed the peacock purse and handed it over to Iris, Hera's winged servant and the goddess of the rainbow. With shiny wings, Iris flew Jen's gift to the goddess of marriage and family. Then Pete took Jen's hand and, together, they left Mount Olympus.

CHAPTER SEVEN

Lake Volta

Jen followed Pete back to his rooms—to Than's old rooms, where Pete and Tizzie now lived together. "You were amazing, man. Thanks for saving my life."

He grinned. "You still talk like a mortal."

Jen sat at the small golden table and tried not to blush in front of her brother. "Like you don't sometimes forget, too?"

"It's pretty hard for me to forget."

Jen sensed that Pete wasn't happy. "What's up, Pete? Are you having second thoughts?"

"No." He sat across from her. "It's worth it—being Death. It means I get to be with Tizzie."

"You two make a great couple."

"Thanks. I love hanging out with her."

"What do y'all do together?"

"Well, I mostly follow her around, like a love-sick puppy."

They both laughed.

Then he added, "But, seriously, I do go with her to avenge the dead. It helps, you know what I mean?"

"Nuh-uh."

"My job is so…loathsome. That's the only word I can think of. Seriously. I don't know how Than did it for so long."

"Are you that miserable?"

"Like I said. It's worth it. Plus, when I find souls who've been wrongfully murdered, especially if it was in a truly heinous way, I get great satisfaction in alerting Tizzie and going after the culprit with her. It's not my duty to be the punisher, but I love watching."

Jen guessed she understood, though she wasn't sure she could ever stomach it herself. "I just wish you were happier with your own duties."

Pete shrugged. "Somebody's got to do it. But I do wish I took as much pleasure in my work as Tizzie takes in hers."

"Maybe one day you'll feel differently."

He shot her a look across the table expressing his doubt.

"Or not," she added.

He smiled. "No worries. I'm good. Really." Then he met her eyes and asked, "What about you?"

Jen wanted to tell him that she absolutely loved her duties. Saving children from their abusers made her feel powerful and satisfied. But she didn't want to rub it in Pete's face, so she just said, "I'm good, too."

Later that evening, Jen met Scylla in the Gulf of Guinea, near the coast of Lome, in West Africa. Apparently, Scylla liked neither to fly nor to god travel and preferred to swim everywhere she went. The plan was to swim upriver to Lake Volta, where the shipping companies would begin their evening runs.

Jen rode on Stormy's back, invisible to mortal eyes. She hovered above the water where Scylla's six long necks emerged from the water. The rest of the monster was hidden below the surface. Jen wondered if Scylla was in invisibility mode, too, or if mortals could see her.

"Did you bring the vials?" Scylla screeched up at her, where Jen hovered on Stormy's back.

Jen patted the bag she had strapped across the front of her. "There's at least a dozen in here."

"I want to look through them and smell them first," Scylla said.

Jen had already agreed to this. Initially, Scylla wanted to use the potion before swamping the boats, but Jen pointed out that she would be more effective as a monster. Scylla had begrudgingly agreed, saying that she supposed she would enjoy one last escapade in her true form.

Stormy lowered himself into the water. Jen could tell he was nervous, especially after what he'd witnessed the Maenads do to Sugar.

"It's okay, boy," Jen murmured near his ear. "We can trust her."

Jen hoped she was right about Scylla.

One of Scylla's center necks bent down, and the one eye peered closely at Jen. "Why are you doing this for me? You could have had anyone help you destroy these fishing companies. You didn't need to make this deal with me."

Jen swallowed hard and said, "Everyone deserves a chance to overcome their past and be who they want to be."

Scylla said nothing more as she waited for Jen to hand over the first vial.

The monster took one look at the glass bottle and shook all six heads. "I thought I told you the formula was green."

"No, you didn't."

"Well, it is. Yellowish green."

Jen rummaged through the vials, desperate to find the right one. Please be in here, she thought as she came across potions that were purple, black, clear, red, and orange. Who knew what these suckers could do to a person? At the very bottom, she found the smallest one. Yes! Its contents resembled lemon-lime soda. "Aha."

Scylla took the vial and uncorked the stopper to sniff the solution inside. "This is it! This is the one!"

"You promised to drink it *after*," Jen reminded her.

Scylla tucked the vial away in the folds of her skin above the barking dogs at her waist. Then she said, "Here come the boats. Where's Hera?"

The boats eased from the bank onto the lake. Jen studied the sky, hoping for a sign. The plan would fail if Hera didn't do her part.

"I don't know," Jen said, worried. "She should be here by now."

Therese sat on the couch between Hermie and Hestie reading some of her favorite stories. Clifford curled up in Hermie's lap getting his ears scratched. Much to Therese's amazement, the twins were beginning to recognize the patterns of letters and words and had begun to read simple sentences on their own.

One of Therese's favorite children's stories was *The Monster at the End of This Book*, featuring Grover from Sesame Street. In his dramatic way, Grover begged the reader not to turn the page, so as to avoid coming to the monster at the end, but the twins laughed and insisted that each page be turned.

Hermie took over and read, "You turned the page!"

Therese kissed his cheek. "You kids are so smart!"

Hestie shook her head. "We just have it memorized."

Hermie nodded. "Yeah. I just know what it says already."

"You're smart *and* honest." Therese kissed Hestie's cheek, too.

Than walked in from the garage, where they parked their Lamborghinis. The cars were a bit extravagant for Therese's taste, but they were gifts from Aphrodite, and who could turn down a goddess? Plus, they were reminders of the fun time they had had with Hermes a few years ago when he'd taught each of them how to drive.

Therese looked up and gave Than a smile. His hair, t-shirt, and jeans were wet, as usual. Thank goodness for leather seats.

And Therese never got tired of the view.

"Daddy!" the kids shouted, rushing from the couch.

Clifford followed and greeted Than by jumping up on his shins.

The kids literally leapt onto him—Hestie into his arms and Hermie onto Than's back.

"You're getting all wet!" Than warned, just like he did every day.

But the kids didn't care.

"Watch out for his broken arm!" Therese called out.

"Sorry!" Hestie said.

"It's fine," Than assured them. "This cast is impenetrable."

Therese got up from the couch and followed them into the kitchen. "I still can't believe you went back to work already, or that your boss allowed it."

"The river is slow this time of year. It was nothing."

They visited with him as he ate his lunch over the kitchen sink, as usual. The kids still wore their new Batman and Robin costumes, and they ran around him, showing off. Later, while Than showered, the kids went down for their afternoon nap.

Therese put the leftover lunch away and washed the dishes—again. As much as she loved this mortal life, this chance to be with her children and watch them grow, she had to admit that she'd do anything—anything but leave her children—to be a goddess again.

A few minutes later, Than came into the kitchen from the shower in fresh jeans and a blue button-down shirt that brought out the blue in his eyes.

She was surprised he hadn't needed her help. "Your arm must be feeling better."

"I can use my fingers without much pain."

"It must be a drag not to be able to heal in a matter of hours, like in the old days."

They rarely talked about what they had given up. She supposed it was even more painful for him, since he had been a god for his entire life.

"What's wrong?" he asked, sensing her mood.

"Jen was here earlier."

He came up behind her at the kitchen sink and wrapped his good arm around her waist. She looked out the window at her favorite red birds. She didn't want them to hear what she was about to say, so she turned away from the window, to face Than.

"Is she okay?" he asked.

Therese told him about Jen's need to prove herself to the Under-world gods, about Therese's suggestion that she go to Hera for help.

"That was good advice," he said. "So what's really bothering you?"

"She asked me if I miss it."

Than frowned.

She grabbed his good hand and squeezed it. "I love my life here with you and the kids. I really do."

"But?"

Tears stung her eyes. "I do miss it. I miss it so much!"

He cupped the back of her head and pulled her in close. She cried against his chest, feeling small and selfish. She hadn't meant to break down like this, wanting to be strong for him. But she was weak in every way imaginable.

The first of the fishing boats began casting nets into the big, wide lake. Jen could see five to six little boys and girls already hard at work. First they threw the nets into the water. Then they dragged them back into the boat. As some of the children pulled up the nets, others untangled the fish that came up with them and dropped the fish into buckets.

More boats got to work as well. When Jen heard shouting come from one of them, she turned to see a man ordering a boy to dive into the water to untangle a net that was hung up on the bottom of the lake. The boy refused, and the man slapped him with the end of a paddle. The boy fell overboard.

Jen disintegrated and swam to the unconscious boy as she said to Scylla, "We have to do this now, with or without Hera."

Scylla didn't need to be told twice. Making herself visible to mortals, she reared her massive body up from the water and screeched an ear-splitting sound that made Jen shudder. Jen disintegrated all over the lake, ready to catch the children as Scylla upturned the boats with her giant pincers.

As Jen had expected, the children, along with their masters, were terrified; but, as Jen came upon each of the trembling boys and girls that plunged into the cold water, she assured them, in their native tongue—which was an English dialect—that this was a rescue mission.

Over and over, each little child asked with astonishment, "You're taking me home?"

"Yes," she said. "Come with me."

Then, each child promptly fell asleep in her arms.

Jen swam with each child to the place where Hera was supposed to meet her. She treaded in the water, trying her best to warm each of the forty-three children she held in her arms. If she could fly, she might succeed without Hera, but she didn't dare risk dropping the children back into the lake and waking them from their slumber.

Meanwhile, Scylla rounded up the older men and boys—the slave masters—and took them as her prisoners. Holding them in her tentacles, she swam from the lake, down the river, and back out to sea to her cave, where they were to meet their punishment. The next morning, Scylla would release them, with warnings that they would die if they took anymore children into slavery. They would be left on their own to find their way back to their villages.

Most of the children were without shoes. A few wore raggedy sandals. All wore dingy shorts, and while the few girls had shirts, nearly all the boys were shirtless.

Just when Jen was about to give up on Hera, the rainbow appeared in the sky, and Iris flew along the huge arch, down into the lake, where the end of the rainbow dipped into the water. She flew to Jen and helped each of the children onto her rainbow bridge, saying, "Come along, dearies. It's time to go home."

The faces of the children quickly transformed from expressions of sleepy bewilderment to those of wonder and excitement as they boarded the rainbow, its bright, translucent colors shooting through the air. The children stared with delight at the small, winged goddess who helped them board, and then, as they climbed up the giant arch, gazed below them at the lake from the wide, blue sky. More than one of the kids asked if they had died and were entering heaven.

"No," Iris replied. "We're taking you home."

Keeping her distance so as not to make them sleepy, Jen followed the last of the kids into the rainbow, where Hera asked each child for the name of their village and their parents' surname. Over the course of the next few hours, they delivered children to their homes, where each household received a lecture from Hera about what selling a child into slavery really meant: no education or proper meals—only abuse and often death. Most of the parents were shocked and grateful to have their children back, but some didn't know how they would feed them. A single mother with no work begged the goddess to help her. A grandmother, whose daughter had died giving birth, was too old to keep her granddaughter. An uncle, who had survived a terrible storm that had killed his sister, barely had enough for his own children to eat, let alone the nephews the goddess had brought back to him. Jen realized that the parents and guardians had sold their children out of desperation. They had no means to take care of them.

Jen remained in the rainbow, so as not to put the mortals to sleep, but she could see and hear all that happened.

One of the villagers told Hera about a school charity that might take some of the children that no one wanted. The charity was able to take all but the youngest—a three-year-old boy. It was the same child who'd been praying to Jen.

"He's too young for our program," a stern-looking woman explained.

"Is there an orphanage he can go to?" Hera asked.

"Not in this region."

Hera returned to the rainbow with the boy no one wanted.

"I'm afraid he's your problem now," she said to Jen. "I've done all I can."

Jen took the child into her arms, and his sad, frightened eyes immediately closed as he was overcome with sleep.

"There, there," Jen whispered. "I'll think of something. Don't you worry."

But, at the moment, she had no idea what she was going to do.

Hip had never been happier to be alive. As soon as his body called to his soul, he merged with it, and the duties of Sleep instantly came upon him.

It was nice to be home! And by home, he meant, of course, in his body.

He disintegrated and flew to the Fields of Asphodel to take over the duties of Sleep from Jen. Sleeping beside her among the white, iridescent flowers was a small child with skin as dark as Tizzie's.

At Hip's arrival, Jen opened her eyes and smiled.

"Hi, Babe," Hip said.

She leapt to her feet and threw herself against him.

He'd forgotten how good she felt.

She returned his eager kisses, which became evermore feverish and desperate. She took his breath away, and he found himself wanting more, never wanting to stop pressing himself against her.

A movement at his feet brought him from his reverie. He looked down at the sleeping child, who had turned onto his side, the elephant in the room—or, er, the fields.

"Who's this?" he asked.

She sucked in her lips, as though she wasn't going to tell him. After a beat, she said, "Now don't get mad."

He groaned.

C H A P T E R   E I G H T

The Boy No One Wanted

While the boy slept in the Asphodel with Hip, Jen rode Stormy through the sky toward her home in Colorado. It felt good to be herself again, without the duties of Sleep. Why should she ever give up riding Stormy, anyway? They were a natural fit, like two peas in a pod.

This train of thought reminded her that Ares had recently left the ranch to return to Mount Olympus, his punishment served. Jen wondered how Bobby was taking it.

Her concern for Bobby didn't thwart the sheer exuberance and pride she felt for having completed a difficult mission. With the help of Scylla, Hera, and Iris—and without the help of the Underworld gods—Jen had saved over forty children from lives of slavery, abuse, and early death. While it was true that there was still one boy who needed a home, she was working on that.

Jen had also helped Scylla become the goddess she had always wanted to be. Soon, Jen would help her face Keto.

But before she faced Scylla's mother, Jen needed to ask a favor of her own.

"You've got to be kidding me, baby girl," her mother said after Jen had made her request. "I just lost Ares, my best worker, and now you want me to take care of a three-year-old who doesn't even speak my language?"

"If you try real hard, you can understand him."

"Baby doll, I've got work to do."

"Please? Just for a few days, while I look for another place for him to live."

"Can't you ask Therese or Carol? They've already got little ones at home. What's one more?"

Jen didn't feel close enough to Carol and Richard to ask them. Besides, they had no clue about the gods and goddesses, and coming up with a logical explanation for the boy's presence wouldn't be easy.

And she couldn't ask Therese. Jen didn't feel right asking such a huge favor of the friend who gave up her immortality. What was Jen gonna say? Excuse me, Therese. I know you're not a goddess anymore. And, even though I'm able to do all the things you wish you could do, I need you to do something for me. Can you babysit this African child who speaks a different dialect of English while I fly across the world on Stormy's back?

Yeah. Right.

Jen couldn't do it.

The thing was, she knew Therese would say yes. But Jen didn't feel right asking.

Ariadne had offered to keep the boy until Jen could find a home, but Jen was afraid the Minotaur would frighten him or that he'd get lost in the labyrinth.

Before leaving her mother's house, Jen went looking for Bobby. She found him grooming Ace in the barn. Mr. Stern—John—was there, too, brushing Sassy. After some small talk, John left to get something from the house, leaving Jen alone with Bobby.

Mr. Stern sure was perceptive, Jen thought. He knew she wanted some time alone with her brother.

"How's Hip?" Bobby asked, since he was aware of what had happened with the Maenads.

"Good as new," she said. "How are you doing?"

"Me?" He gave her a surprised look. "Fine. Why would you ask?"

She took up a brush and began stroking Sassy. "Well, Sugar's gone, and now Ares."

"Jen, I'm a grown man now. You do realize that?"

She looked at him. He was taller than she was, and even though his boyish face and blond, bowl-cut hair was the same, his body was wider and more muscular. In fact, he reminded her of Pete. They could be twins.

"I'm just sorry I took Sugar into danger," Jen said.

"You didn't know that would happen," he said. "Besides, if it hadn't been Sugar, it might have been Therese or Than. Sugar was a hero."

Jen gave him a somber smile. "Yes, she was."

"And I liked Ares," Bobby said, "but he sure liked to talk a lot. Wore me out sometimes."

"Really? What about?"

"Mostly himself."

Jen busted out laughing.

"It was interesting, usually," Bobby continued. "All the battles he ever fought in, all the brave deeds he ever did. It made me think maybe I should go off on an adventure."

"College would be an adventure," Jen said.

"Nah. Mom and John need me here."

"They could get on without you. Hire someone."

"*You* didn't go. Why should *I*?"

"I never wanted to," she said. "But you're not me."

Bobby didn't say anything. He didn't have to. Jen knew what he was thinking. He wanted to go to college and become a veterinarian. It had been his life-long dream.

"You can always come back here when you're done," Jen added.

"I'll think about it," he finally said, though it felt to Jen like he just wanted to get her off his back.

She brushed Sassy a while longer as feelings of nostalgia washed over her. Tears welled in her eyes, and when she sniffed, she said something about her allergies.

"Gods have allergies?" Bobby teased.

Darn. He'd called her bluff.

"So what brought you home?" he asked. "Did you come all this way just to check up on me?"

"No, as a matter of fact, I did not." She told him about her mission and the little boy no one wanted.

"Why don't you keep him yourself?" Bobby said.

"Yeah, right."

"I'm serious. Why not?"

Jen looked over the horse at Bobby's face for signs of sarcasm and found none. "Well, even if I could—and I can't, because Zeus won't allow it—I'd make a terrible mom."

"That's the stupidest thing I've ever heard."

Jen raised her brows. "Seriously?"

When he didn't reply, she asked, "You really think I'd make a good mother?"

"The best," he said. "I mean, I know we fought a lot—that's what brothers and sisters do—but you also looked out for me, just like you're doing today."

Jen couldn't believe her ears. This was probably the first time in her life her brother ever paid her a genuine compliment. "Wow. Thanks, Bobby."

"What's his name?" he asked.

"Poor little guy doesn't know. His brother called him *Muggie*. That means *tiny bug*."

"Where's his brother?"

"Dead. He was told to jump in the lake to untangle a fishing net, and he never came back up."

"Man. That's rough."

"Yeah. Tell me about it."

They were quiet for a minute. Jen wondered if Bobby was thinking of Pete.

Then Jen added, "Muggie is such a cute, sweet boy. Such a gentle little guy. Kind of reminds me of you when you were little."

Bobby stepped away from Ace to start working on Hershey, a brown gelding the color of chocolate. "You're not that much older than me."

"Still. I remember."

Bobby blushed and gave her a smile. "How long you stayin'?"

"I gotta go. But I'll be back soon."

Jen said goodbye to Bobby and to the horses and then went inside once more to say goodbye to her mom and to John. Then she hopped onto Stormy, and away they flew.

As much as Hip felt sorry for the little African boy Jen had rescued, he hadn't expected to have to babysit the moment he was free from Tartarus. He gazed down at the sleeping form curled beside him in the Asphodel and wondered what nightmares must be plaguing the boy no one wanted. Out of both pity and curiosity, Hip decided to find out.

He wasn't surprised to discover the setting of the dream to be Lake Volta, but he *was* surprised to see the boy flying above the water, holding Iris's hands, the two of them twirling in the air in a dance with an enormous rainbow arched across the bright sky. Iris's golden wings fluttered at her back. The boy smiled from ear to ear. Bluebirds twittered around them, singing a lively tune.

Iris looked so much like her natural self that at first Hip wondered how Hera's messenger goddess had entered his realm without him knowing. But when both Jen and Hera appeared on the scene and joined hands with the boy and Iris, Hip realized what was happening.

The boy was a lucid dreamer, and he was commanding the figments.

Curious to see what the boy would do next, Hip watched on from afar. He chuckled when sausages and loaves of bread descended from the clouds and found their way into the boy's eager hands. The gods fell away, and now the boy sat at a golden table with another boy, maybe three years older, whom he called *Bru*, which meant *Brother*.

The two boys ate the bread and sausages and then bowls and bowls of sponge pudding, until their stomachs were bulging, and they could eat no more. Then Bru picked up a ball, and the table fell away as they tossed the ball back and forth to one another in the grass, laughing as they each tried to throw faster and harder than the other.

Wanting to test the skills of the boy, Hip summoned a figment in the form of a viper and commanded it to attack the image of Bru, but before the viper struck, Muggie, as his brother called him, transformed into a gigantic hawk and plucked the viper from the grass, tossing him into the lake.

Further testing the boy, Hip turned the viper into a boar that barreled toward the hawk from the lake. The hawk became a panther and pierced the pig flesh with sharp teeth. Hip made the boar into a bear, and, to Hip's astonishment, the boy who was a panther became a man with a rifle. He shot the bear.

Then, on his own, the boy transformed the bear into his slave master, dead from the gunshot wound at his chest, where a gaping, bloody hole was still visible. The boy carried his slave master to a wooden crate and gingerly laid him to rest. Then the boy told the dead man to go to hell.

Hip turned the slave master into the dead body of Muggie's brother, to see what the boy would do.

Tears sprang to the boy's eyes, and he cried out, "Jislaaik!"

Hip recognized the expression of bewilderment and confusion.

Then drying his eyes, Muggie resurrected his brother, and the two began throwing the ball once more in the grass.

Hip observed the boy with awe. There was only one mortal whom Hip had ever seen with such amazing powers in the Dreamworld, and she was now married to his brother.

CHAPTER NINE

Play Time

When Jen returned to the Fields of Asphodel, she was moved with tenderness by the sight of Muggie curled up next to Hip. The thought of having a child didn't seem so awful at the moment; it might even be nice.

Hip opened his eyes and smiled up at her. "Hey, pretty lady."

"Hey, handsome."

"As much as I want to hold you for a very long time, this little munchkin needs food and drink," Hip said. "I think he's in danger of dehydration."

Jen frowned. "Oh, gosh. What should I do?"

"Your mom won't take him?"

"She's got too much work to do."

"What about Therese?"

Jen sighed. "I can't ask her to look after him, but maybe she'll help me feed him."

Hip looked at her puzzled, praying, *Why can't she look after him for a few days?*

She's already done so much for me, and at a great cost.

Not just for you. For herself and Than. For the twins.

But she's given up so much. I can tell she's depressed about it.

Jen took the little boy in her arms and said, "I'll go for a visit and get him fed. I'll see you later, okay?"

Before she left, Hip stroked the sleeping boy's cheek. "He's a lucid dreamer. Even stronger than Therese. I'll definitely be visiting this little guy again. He's pretty entertaining. Like a little chameleon."

Jen kissed Muggie's cheek and frowned. "What if I don't find him a home?"

"Let's cross that bridge when we get to it, Babe, Okay?" He stroked her cheek in the same way he had just stroked the boy's.

"Okay."

Therese was shocked when Jen appeared to her for the third time in a single week. "Wow!" she said. "It almost feels like you never moved!" Then she noticed the child in Jen's arms. "Who's this?"

"Can we come in?" Jen asked at the front door.

"Of course!"

Therese opened the door and watched with astonishment as her best friend stepped over the Legos and building blocks scattered on the living room floor and went directly to the kitchen, where Jen helped the boy to a glass of water. The boy drank greedily as water dripped down his chin and onto his bare chest.

"He's starving and thirsty," Jen explained. "Do you have any food we can feed him?"

It was mid-morning. "Breakfast or lunch?"

"Anything you have a lot of."

"Is mac and cheese okay?" Therese asked, still a bit puzzled by Jen's arrival with the little boy on her hip.

"That would be perfect," Jen said before turning to the boy and saying something in a language Therese could barely understand.

Therese opened the fridge and retrieved yesterday's leftover mac and cheese. After warming it up, she put it on a plate with a fork and then joined Jen and the boy at the kitchen table. The plate was clean in no time.

"He really was starving," Therese said.

The boy smiled at her. "Lekker, tannie. Thanks." He took another long drink of water from his cup.

"He says it's delicious and thank you," Jen explained to Therese.

Therese nodded and then asked the boy, "Would you like more?"

"Ja?" the boy's eyes widened with disbelief. "Ag, am I dreaming? Dis is to die for!"

Therese got up and put the remaining mac in cheese, along with a couple of wieners, into the microwave.

While they warmed, Jen asked, "Where are the twins?"

"Taking a morning nap. They'll be up soon."

"Could Muggie and I stay and visit awhile?"

Therese threw her arms in the air, a rush of happiness overcoming her. "Do you have to ask?" The only people who ever visited her anymore were her aunt and uncle. Todd and Ray, two of her very best friends, had gone out of town for college. Hermes had come by a few times, as had Persephone, but they had mainly come to see Than.

Jen grinned at Therese and then took a napkin to Muggie's chin, which made the boy smile gleefully. He seemed to enjoy being cared for.

As Therese took the second helping of food from the microwave and returned to the table, she asked, "So tell me what's going on."

"We'll talk later, while the kids play."

Therese understood, giving Jen a reassuring nod.

Jen picked up one of the hotdogs and said, "Muggie, take a hap of this."

The boy leaned over and took a bite. His face lit up as he chewed and swallowed. "Mmm. Blimmin lekker, tannie!"

Jen laughed. "He likes it."

"I can tell."

Hip gazed affectionately down at Jen from afar, where he hovered over the San Juan Mountains of Colorado. He hadn't meant to spy, but he had missed her and had wanted badly to see her.

He enjoyed watching her care for the little boy. When he imagined how she might be with a child of their own, sadness swept over him. He could think of nothing he could say or do that would ever change Zeus's mind. There could be no more gods. The pantheon was already complicated enough and delicately balanced. As he watched Jen wipe Muggie's chin and kiss his cheek, Hip sighed. Then, with a heavy heart, he flew away.

When the twins woke up from their nap, they ran like lightning down the stairs to the living room with Clifford ambling behind them but stopped short when they saw the boy. Muggie had already made himself comfortable on the living room floor, where he'd been building things out of Legos. Jen wondered what the twins were thinking as she jumped up from the couch to hug them and to pet Clifford between the ears.

"I brought you a friend to play with," she said. "This is Muggie."

"Hi," Hermie said as Hestie put her finger in her mouth.

"What's wrong, Hestie?" Therese asked.

"Those are *our* toys, Mommy," she said. "Does Muggie know that?"

Before Therese could answer, Muggie turned to Jen and asked, "Hey? What did she say, tannie?"

"I said those are our toys," Hestie repeated, using Muggie's dialect.

"Eish! I know! Chill, kugel!" Muggie said. "Your dog is cute."

"What's a kugel?" Hestie asked.

"Ag, a girl who hogs her toys," Muggie replied.

"What are they saying?" Therese asked.

Jen looked at Hestie with surprise. "You can understand him? You can speak like him?"

Hestie put her finger back into her mouth and gave Jen a blank look.

"His English is very different from ours," Therese explained to Hestie. "We're just surprised you can understand it."

"It sounds the same to me, Mommy," Hermie said.

"Me, too," Hestie said.

"Well, that's interesting," Jen said to Therese. "Maybe language is one of their talents."

"I guess so. They amaze me every day." Therese curled one of Hestie's pig tails around her finger. "We can share our toys, can't we?"

Hestie nodded. "But can Hermie and I play, too?"

"Of course," Therese said.

The twins sat on the floor near Muggie. It wasn't long before the three of them were playing like old friends, even speaking the same language. Clifford sat close to Muggie, too, since the boy kept stroking his back and kissing his head, as though he were unused to being around pets. While they were distracted, Jen told Therese the story of how Muggie came to be in her possession.

When Jen had finished, Therese asked, "So where will you take him? Back to Africa?"

Jen shrugged. "I guess I could go to one of the bigger cities, where people have money. But I want to be sure it's a good home, you know? He's been through so much. I can't just dump him anywhere."

"Maybe we should give him a bath and buy him some new clothes and shoes," Therese pointed out. "Make him more presentable."

"That's actually a great idea." Jen's mood brightened. "Lunch and shopping in Durango?"

"Sounds like a plan!"

They put all three kids in the tub and shampooed their hair. Muggie enjoyed playing with the plastic fish and other bath toys and squirting colorful foam on the wall over the tub, but when the twins wrote their names on the wall and told Muggie to do the same, Muggie shook his head. Jen was about to explain that Muggie didn't know how to read and write when Hestie started teaching him.

"You sound it out," the little girl said. "Mmma, that means M."

Hestie wrote the letter on the wall.

"Bakgat!" the boy said, which meant, "Awesome!"

"What comes after M, Aunt Jen?" Hestie asked.

Jen helped her to spell it out in the green foam.

"See?" Hestie said. "That spells Muggie. That's you."

The boy laughed.

Therese, who was sitting on the lid of the commode, looked down at Jen, where she knelt on a bathmat on the floor. "You're pretty good at this mothering thing."

"It's funny you should say that," Jen said. "Hip asked me to keep an open mind."

"Why? Zeus won't allow it anyway."

"That's what I told him."

"Besides, I thought you said you didn't want kids."

Jen was quiet for a moment as she watched little Muggie.

"Jen?" Therese asked. "You okay?"

"I didn't think I did, but now…I kind of do."

Therese frowned. "I'm sorry, girlfriend."

Jen shook her head, suddenly feeling selfish. What did she have to whine about? She was a goddess, something Jen suspected Therese wished she could be again, too.

Why did it always seem like the grass was greener on the other side?

While the twins got dressed, Jen held Muggie in one towel while she patted his hair dry with another. Therese made a quick trip to Carol's to borrow a t-shirt, pair of shorts, and flip-flops from Lynn, who was a little bigger than Muggie, but not by much. Then they climbed into Therese's Lamborghini and headed to town.

Hip followed Selene's silver chariot over the dark side of the earth, over Russia and the Middle East, bringing sleep to the mortals who needed it. Selene's brother, Helios, was always on the opposite side of the world, and they made these rotations together almost constantly, except that, unlike the sun and moon Titans, Hip was disintegrated across the perimeter to the north and the south, so that he could better see the mortals and bring sleep to the right ones. The three of them had been making these rotations for as long as Hip could remember, taking very few breaks to eat and sleep. And even while he slept, Hip worked in the Dreamworld, so that he was almost always in motion, doing something somewhere. For most of his life, Hip liked it this way. Life was rarely boring for him—not like the life Than, and now Pete, had to lead. But lately, he wished things could slow down.

Hours later, when he reached the eastern parts of Africa and made his way, as slowly as Selene, across the night sky, he reflected on the little boy Jen had saved from slavery and how nice it had been to feel like a father for a short while.

He hadn't been contemplating this for long when his thoughts were interrupted by a distressful prayer from Ares. The god of war called out to all gods for emergency assistance.

I'm trapped in a North Alaskan gorge, Ares said telepathically to all the gods who could hear him. *I chased one of the Giants over the Brooks Range, and now he's got me trapped near a granite spire called Shot Tower in the Arrigetch Peaks.*

Why can't you god-travel out of there? Hip asked as he disintegrated and flew in that direction.

Because the Giant's eaten one of my legs, and I won't leave without it.

CHAPTER TEN

Ares Falls

When Hip arrived in the cold skies over the northern mountains of Alaska, he didn't have to look far to find Ares, because half of the Olympians were already there, battling against two ferocious Giants. The beasts were twins—each with three green, scaly dragon heads, at least a hundred legs with sharp claws on each foot, and long serpent tails that whipped up from behind them, like enormous scorpion stingers. Along their backs stood rows of red spikes, and through their sharp teeth, along with raging fire, came the most horrendous shrieks, loud enough to make the mountains tremble. Hypnos could barely think straight as he bore the shrill, painful cries of the beasts and flew to fight alongside Hera, Athena, Artemis, Apollo, Hephaestus, Hermes, and Poseidon.

The gods hovered in the air above the beasts, who seemed incapable of flight, or the battle would have been lost by now. The Giants' hundred legs straddled the expanse of the gorge, where Ares lay trapped beneath. Hip could sense that the god of war was exhausted, like a jarred moth that had been fighting against the glass for too long.

Apollo and Artemis shot one arrow after another at the monsters, but their arrowheads seemed ineffectual against the scaly skin of the Giants. Although the twins aimed at the eyes, snouts, and mouths, the heads were in constant movement and were not easy targets.

The other gods dodged the scorpion-like tails and the hot red fire that blew from their mouths, trying to lodge their spears into the backs or necks of the monsters, but the beasts were too quick, nearly as fast as any god. Even Poseidon's trident wasn't powerful enough to paralyze them—though one of the heads rolled its eyes back after a direct hit, and its tongue hung limp from its mouth. Although the other two heads seemed unaffected, Athena took this opportunity to strike.

She drove her spear into the back of the injured beast. Then its tail lashed out against her and threw her thousands of feet across the sky. Hypnos disintegrated into thirty in her direction and was able to stop her from slamming into one of the granite mountaintops. She thanked him as they both hastened back to battle.

When Apollo's arrow found one of the good eyes of the already injured beast, the other monster abandoned its brother. It leapt from the mountain, and, for a moment, seemed to be flying.

Don't let him get away! Ares prayed to them telepathically. *I don't know which beast swallowed my leg!*

While Athena, Apollo, Hera, and Poseidon continued to fight the injured Giant still straddling the gorge over Ares, Hip and the others chased after its twin. Hip tried with all his might to put the Giant into the deep boon of sleep, but the monster kept running. Artemis shot arrow after arrow, Hermes conjured spear after spear, and Hephaestus threw ax after ax. Hip disintegrated into the hundreds and god-traveled at a point in the mountains he estimated the beast would soon arrive, creating a wall with which he hoped to slow it down.

Hip sucked in air as the enormous Giant charged him. Each of his fragmented selves conjured a spear and stood at the ready. Although he launched most of the spears at the Giant, a few of them finding their marks, at least ten of his fragmented selves were trampled by the hundred feet and five hundred claws of the beast. Hip had no choice but to integrate into the most injured one of himself, so that he could better heal, momentarily leaving his duties of Sleep. It took only a few minutes to overcome the bruising and cut skin, but by the time he resumed his power of disintegration, the monstrous beast was gone. The other gods had lost track of him, so they returned to the gorge to help the others.

Aphrodite was among them, and she was viciously cutting open the belly of the enormous Giant in search of Ares's leg. The other gods helped, but none had the fierce determination of Aphrodite. Ares was the love of her life, and Hip could see the angry tears rolling down her cheeks.

Apollo attended to Ares as the others splayed the monster open on the mountaintop. After hours of searching the beast's remains, there was no sign of the leg belonging to the god of war.

Jen returned to the Fields of Asphodel with Muggie on Stormy's back from a day of lunching and shopping in Durango with her best friend. She needed to ask Hip to watch the boy so she could go back to her duties. Up at the top of her list of priorities was helping Scylla face her mother, and, as much as she loved spending time with Muggie, she couldn't very well take him with her.

She'd actually taken the boy over Africa on the way back, intending to study the mortals below for signs of a good home. She'd even pointed out a few of the nicer houses to him, and they'd watched the families through the windows. But she wasn't ready to part with him just yet. In fact, the thought of it made her feel strangely sad and empty inside—it was a new and unfamiliar feeling.

Muggie had been well-behaved during their outing with Therese and her twins. Jen hadn't known what to expect of such a young boy who couldn't remember his mother or father, who had watched his brother die, and who had been sorely abused and mistreated. But he was polite and kind and happy, and he showed tremendous gratitude for the new clothes and shoes that Jen had bought for him. When she offered to buy him multiple sets of clothes, he turned her down, saying he didn't need more than two shirts, two pants, and two underpants, because while he wore one set, he would wash the other.

But he hadn't turned down her offer to buy him a toy. He told her that the only thing he had ever owned of his very own (even his clothes had been shared) had been a toothbrush. He said it had been given to him by a charity woman—she'd brought toothbrushes for all the slave children. And he said he used to play with it and had given it a name. It was his imaginary friend for weeks, and, one day, when he couldn't find it, he'd cried for hours.

Jen bought him another toothbrush, the same sky-blue color as his first, which made him spring tears of joy; and, he also let her buy him a plush toy dragon. He made a swishing sound with his mouth as he held the dragon aloft in one hand and the toothbrush aloft in the other, flying them though the air from the ends of his arms. Jen had asked what he was pretending, and he'd said that the toothbrush was the dragon's brother, and they were flying wherever they liked.

When Jen found Hip lying among the iridescent flowers, he opened his eyes and gave her a somber smile. Muggie immediately fell asleep in her arms, cuddling the only two things he possessed in the world besides his new clothes and shoes.

"What's wrong?" she asked Hip.

"Ares went after the Giants, and one of them swallowed his leg," Hip said. "I helped fight the beasts, but the one with the leg ran off, and we lost track of him."

"Can Ares grow another one?" she asked.

"No. Gods can heal and regenerate skin and even some organ tissue, but we can't grow entire limbs." Then he added, "Ares went a whole year without his powers. What made him think he could just jump into battle on his first day back?"

Jen slumped on the ground beside him, holding Muggie against her. "What's he going to do now?"

"We're discussing it on Mount Olympus." Hip stroked Muggie's soft, clean hair and added, "Looks like someone had a bath."

"We went shopping after," she said. "He's such a sweet boy."

"He really is a special little guy," Hip agreed. "I enjoy watching him in the Dreamworld. He's a little chameleon. He can change himself into anything."

"What's he doing now?"

"He's flying as a dragon. And he's turned one figment into that dragon toy and another into that toothbrush—don't ask me why. They're soaring over the African coast, having a grand old time."

Jen laughed and told him what Muggie had said about his first toothbrush.

"Poor little thing," Hip said. "I almost wish we didn't have to give him back."

Jen's breath caught. She'd been thinking the same thing all day. Was Hip serious? Or just making a casual remark. "I feel the same way," she said bravely, anxious for his reaction.

Hip's face transformed into an expression of utter excitement. His smile cracked his face in half. "Are you serious?"

"Yes, but what's the use? We can't keep him here in the Underworld. He needs other mortals, access to normal food, to an education, doesn't he?"

Hip's smile vanished. "Maybe you're right. I don't know. We've never tried to keep a mortal here."

"Therese *wanted* to stay, but the prophecy said the twins had to be up there, in the Upperworld. Otherwise, would Hades have allowed it?"

"I could ask him about it," Hip offered. "I mean, it wouldn't hurt to ask, right?"

She leaned over the boy in her lap to kiss her husband. "Right."

While Hip talked with Jen in the Fields of Asphodel, he was also on Mount Olympus with the other warriors who had fought against the

Giants, reporting to Zeus and to the other Olympians. Ares insisted on being present, even though he was still in grave pain and in even worse spirits. He lay on a golden couch in front of his throne with his head on Aphrodite's lap. He wore a bloody bandage around the stump near his right hip that wasn't easy on the eyes. His skin was much paler than it usually was, in spite of the tan he'd gotten over the summer in Colorado. He had the appearance of someone who was about to die.

Hip knew Ares was fighting to hold onto his soul. The god of war may be useless at the moment, but if his body relinquished its soul, it would be at least a week—and maybe longer—before the body called for it again.

"We must comb every inch of the earth," Hera said, after Zeus had heard the full story.

"And we start in the mountains above the Arctic Circle," Apollo suggested.

Artemis stood up. "We should spread out. The beast might be all the way down in the Yukon by now."

"Or even further," Hephaestus said.

"The thing was fast enough," Hip added. "Who knows how far it's gone?"

"Which is exactly why we need *you*, Hypnos," Zeus said, pointing a finger at him. "We need your power of disintegration so that you can cover the entire globe at once, leaving no stone unturned, no nook or cranny unexplored."

Back in the Asphodel, Jen had just told Hip that she wanted to keep Muggie, too.

"What's that smile about?" Athena asked him on Mount Olympus.

Hip waved a hand. "I was responding to something somewhere else. Forgive me."

"Are you so easily distracted?" Hera demanded. "Maybe he won't be as helpful as we'd hoped."

"And if he gets partially eaten like your son?" Persephone asked. "Why should he go alone? What about Pete?"

"Pete has no fighting skills," Athena said. "He'll only endanger himself and the rest of us."

"I need someone to get Ares's leg back!" Aphrodite moaned.

"What if Hecate trades duties with Pete?" Hestia suggested.

"No!" Hermes and Demeter said at the same time.

"We only need one of the disintegrating gods," Hermes added.

"Why should Hip, alone, take all the risk?" Persephone argued. "Not that I want my dear Hecate in danger, either."

"I will take the duties of Death," Hermes offered.

Zeus frowned. "But you're the fastest among us, and I need you to relay important communications when we can't reach one another otherwise."

Hermes lifted his hands in the air. "With the power of disintegration, I could do both."

Hera shook her head. "Not if something goes wrong."

"I have a proposition for you," Hip said, turning to face Zeus.

Zeus's brows shot up. "A proposition? What is it?"

All eyes fell on Hypnos. He couldn't believe what he was about to say. Had he gone mad?

Despite the fear coursing through his veins, there was also joy, excitement, hope.

"I'll do everything in my power to track down the Giant," Hip said. "And I'll do whatever it takes to get back Ares's leg, on one condition."

Hera crossed her arms. "We're listening."

"During your negotiations with the Athena Alliance, you agreed to the terms with a demand of your own," Hip said.

"You cannot sire a child, Hypnos," Zeus said.

Hip shook his head. "That's not what I'm asking."

"Then get on with it," Poseidon interjected.

"With Hera's help, Jen rescued a three-year-old mortal boy from a life of slavery and abuse," Hip said.

"I remember the boy," Hera said. "No one wanted him."

"*We* want him," Hip said.

"A mortal can't survive in the Underworld," Hermes pointed out. "There are too many dangers. The Phlegethon, for one, would burn him alive if he ever fell in."

"I want you to make him immortal," Hip said to Zeus.

Gasps filled the room.

"He's got amazing powers in the Dreamworld," Hip quickly continued. "He would be a great help to me if he could take over the duties of dreams so that I could focus on slumber."

"This is out of the question," Zeus said.

Hera turned to her husband and muttered, "But is it?"

"You're in favor of this?" Zeus asked her.

"Look at our son!" Hera cried. "A son for a son is an even trade, no?"

"I don't fancy the idea of a third Underworld deity possessing the power of disintegration," Poseidon said.

"But he wouldn't need it," Hip said. "Since I would still be in charge of slumber, only *I*'d need it—you know, as I go around the globe with Selene. The boy would hang out in the Asphodel. Only his *projection* would disseminate among the realm of dreams."

"He wouldn't be a threat to anyone *there*," Persephone pointed out.

"But how happy could he be living his entire life asleep?" Artemis asked.

"Zeus could grant him the ability to fragment once, like the primordial beings," Apollo pointed out. "The embodiment of Dreams would exist in the Dreamworld while the godly form could exist independently."

Hip wasn't clear on what Apollo was proposing, but it sounded good to him.

"Shall we put it to a vote?" Athena asked her father.

"No," Zeus replied. "This was *my* condition during our negotiations. If it's going to be waived in this instance, it'll be by *me* alone."

Hip tried not to get his hopes up—the hopes that had quickly obliterated the fears—but back in the Fields of Asphodel, he couldn't contain himself.

"What's going on with you?" Jen asked him.

"Hang on a minute, Babe."

Back on Mount Olympus, Zeus pointed his finger again at Hip. "I'll turn the boy into one of us if, and only if, you accomplish *two* things. *One*, bring back my son's leg. And, *two*, find out who or what is responsible for attacking Gaia and releasing the Giants."

CHAPTER ELEVEN

Betrayal

What?" Jen demanded after Hip told her the plan. They stood together in the Fields of Asphodel with Muggie sleeping at their feet. "Are you crazy?"

Hip felt the blood leave his face. "Crazy? What? No. I thought this would make you happy."

"How can you risking your life make me happy?" He'd never seen her face so red.

"Jen, I'm not risking my *life*. I'm a god."

She whipped around, putting her back to him. "You know what I mean." She turned back to face him. "Like you've said before, there are worse things than death."

"I'm not going to let anything happen to me."

"Like Ares?"

"He was out of practice. He'd gone a whole year without his powers. That's not going to happen to me."

She grabbed a fistful of his white shirt and put her face close to his. At first, he thought she was going to kiss him, but, instead, she growled, "You don't know that. And I didn't give up my life on the ranch with my family and friends and all my horses just to be down here spending eternity without you. None of the other gods even *like* me—except Tizzie. She's my only friend, and that's just 'cause she's married to my brother."

"That's not true. Everyone down here likes you."

"That's what you want to believe. They don't think I have what it takes. I can tell. And it's holding me back."

"You *do* have what it takes. *I* know you do. Isn't that enough?" He cupped her angry face in both hands. "Listen to me. I promise I'll be careful. And I'll be here with you the whole time. If things go wrong, I'll reintegrate right back to this spot."

She sighed. "You and I have both been trapped somewhere where we couldn't disintegrate. Just a few days ago, I was stuck in Circe's lair. Remember?"

"That only happened because I was in Tartarus without my body and couldn't keep tabs on you. But this time, you'll have my back, right? And so will my father and sisters."

The expression of anger left her face as tears filled her eyes.

Hip kissed her, quickly, and then added, "This is a chance for us to have a complete family."

"If anything were to happen to you," she murmured. "Oh, Hip."

"Trust me, okay? Have faith in me, even if you don't have faith in yourself."

Silently, she nodded as the tears spilled from her eyes. She threw her arms around his neck, and he held her for several minutes, until she broke away and asked, "What if Muggie doesn't want the same thing for him as we do? Shouldn't we ask him first?"

"But if we ask him and I don't succeed…"

"You just said I should trust you!"

Her hands were trembling again. He took them both in his own and, trying to calm her down, said, "Shh. Listen. I meant you should trust me that I won't get myself eaten. But there's still a good chance that I won't be able to find Ares's leg or figure out who's attacking Gaia. I don't think we should get the boy's hopes up about becoming a god before we know if it's a sure thing."

She bit her lip and then slowly nodded.

"But I'll tell you what," he said. "If I do succeed, we can let it be his choice. If he doesn't want to become like us and take us as his parents, we can go back to finding him a home."

"But then you'll have taken this humungous risk for nothing."

"Not for nothing. For the chance of making our dreams come true. It's worth it."

She looked deeply into his eyes. "I never knew how much having a family meant to you."

"Neither did I. It wasn't until Than and Therese had the twins that it dawned on me."

Jen smiled. "For me, it was spending time with Muggie. I'm not sure I'd have wanted just any child. You know?"

"Yeah. I know."

He reached his lips to hers and sighed against her mouth.

Before he'd met Jen, he never would have believed that this was the man he would want to become. But now that he had her, and he loved her with all his heart, he wanted to take their relationship to the next level. It seemed natural and right to him to become a father, to multiply their little family unit into three. He doubted he would have ever wanted this if it hadn't been for the love he felt for Jen.

He ran his fingers through her hair and pressed his lips hard against hers.

Jen rode on Stormy's back across the Ionian Sea and into Scylla's cave, where she dismounted on the rocky embankment. At first, she didn't see anyone there, but in the next moment a figure appeared from a dark corner. She was a beautiful woman dressed in an orange iridescent gown that clung to her curvy form. Except for thin straps, her pale shoulders were bare, and her long, slender arms were bent at the elbows, her hands on her curvy hips. Her dark hair was in at least a dozen braids that were loosely wound on top of her head. She had a smile on her face, and one of her eyebrows was arched.

Jen took a deep breath. "Scylla?"

"Hard to believe, isn't it?" she said in a throaty voice that wasn't entirely different from the one she'd had before, even though it was softer and more appealing to the ears.

Jen nodded. "It's an amazing transformation. I'm so happy for you. How do you feel?"

"It's nice that who I am on the inside can finally be seen on the outside."

"That's so great." Jen crossed the rocky cavern to the edge of the pool to hug her. Scylla stiffened against her, and when Jen pulled away, she noticed Scylla's face had reddened with a mixture of embarrassment and something else that Jen couldn't read.

Jen added, "You helped save a lot of children. Doesn't it feel good to be on the right side?"

Scylla frowned. "It did feel good. I'll admit that."

Jen felt uneasy. She took a few steps back toward Stormy. "You should be proud of yourself," she said enthusiastically. "You're a hero."

Scylla cocked her head to one side. "What's interesting is that it was the *monster* in me that saved those children."

"It was the *goodness* in you." Jen took another step back. "There's good inside of you, and, like you said, now your outside matches your inside."

"I had a very specific purpose before," Scylla said. "My job was to challenge the sailors that crossed the Messina Straight. Did you know that in order for my transformation to remain permanent, I have to find a new purpose within a few months?"

"I can help you with that," Jen offered just as Stormy gave her a nervous snort.

"That won't be necessary," came a familiar voice from the opening of the cave.

Jen turned to see Keto emerged from the water to her waist. She held a fishing spear with a barbed hook at the end.

"Keto," Jen said with surprise and fear. Her heart pounded against her ribs, and she felt the sudden instinct to run, but she ignored it. "We were just coming to see you. Weren't we, Scylla?"

Jen glanced back at Scylla to find a strange smile on the newly transformed goddess's face.

"Scylla?" Jen asked, realizing too late that she was about to be betrayed. "Don't do this. I can help you."

"My mother offered me a deal I couldn't refuse," Scylla explained. "She said that if I fed you to my father, she'd forgive me for forsaking my birthright by becoming beautiful."

"You don't want to do that," Jen said, barely able to speak or to breathe. She was in full panic mode. She couldn't think. "That isn't who you are."

"Oh, but you're wrong," Keto said. "It's exactly who she is. No matter what she looks like on the outside, she will always be one of us. She will always be a monster."

Jen looked from Scylla to Keto and back at Scylla again. "Don't believe her. It's not true. You told me yourself. You're not a monster! *You get to define who you are!*"

Scylla frowned, and for a moment, Jen thought the new goddess would be persuaded to stand up against her mother. But instead, Scylla said, "If you pray for help, we'll eat Stormy, too. If you want to spare his life, you'll be smart and cooperate."

Stormy snorted again and stepped away from Keto.

Just then, Keto drove her fishing spear into Stormy's flank, and blood spurted from his body as he wailed with pain.

"No!" Jen screamed and raced toward him.

But before she could reach him, he floundered into the water, where a whirlpool sucked him down.

Charybdis! Jen saw the monster's face for the first time. Four circular mouths lined with teeth opened and closed, sucking the water and ripping everything solid that passed through them to shreds. It was horrifying, reminding her of the Kracken from a movie about pirates.

But Stormy was still alive. Jen could see him through the transparent skin of the monster. The horse was flailing and shrieking. Jen wanted to vomit.

"We'll let Stormy go if you cooperate," Keto said.

Jen did the only thing she could. She dove into the water and swam after Stormy.

She tried to pray for help, but the whirlpool that was Charybdis sucked her this way and that, making her lose sight of Stormy. She cried out to him, turning her head side to side, up and down, until another current blasted her, flipped her over, and sucked her even further down, down, down. Her head felt like it was going to explode. She couldn't even hear herself think. She was deaf and blind. And when she finally remembered that she could breathe underwater, she opened her mouth only to find the oxygen gone.

A roar like the sound of a train blasted her eardrums, and that's when she knew where she was. She was inside the belly of the monster.

Dawn had not yet come to the cold, windy mountains of the Brooks Range in northern Alaska, where Hip hovered in search of the Giant that had swallowed Ares's leg. Back in the Fields of Asphodel, Hip held little Muggie while he slept, and, in the Dreamworld, he watched the boy command the figments with amazing control. Hip had enough going on to distract himself from worrying about Jen, but he still worried.

He was disintegrated in the millions around the globe, but he couldn't stop thinking of his wife.

He hadn't liked the idea of her going alone with Stormy to meet with Scylla, but he needed Jen to know he believed in her. And as much as he wanted to reach out in prayer, to ask her if all was well, he knew he should wait for her to report back to him, so she didn't think he doubted her.

Some of the other gods were with him in different parts of the world, helping with the hunt. Hermes had joined him in the eastern mountains of Alaska, Apollo ran along the river with him in central Alaska, and Artemis flew beside him above the Yukon. Athena went with him deeper into Canada, closer to the edge of towns, and Hera flew beside him in the snow over Greenland. So far, they had seen no sign of the Giant.

Of the companions Hip found himself with today, Hermes was by far his favorite. The god of travel and communication, of commerce and thievery, had no trouble making conversation anywhere he went. The stories from his younger days, when he used to play his tricks with much more frequency than in recent decades, were sure to entertain, and Hip enjoyed hearing about them. He was especially fond of the one that Hermes told about Hip's father—about a time Hermes, Hades, and Dionysus played a trick on Poseidon by dressing up his white mares in Persephone's jewels, scarves, and hats. Hermes told it in great detail, including the part where Hades was sent to work on a pig farm. Although Hip had been born by then, he had no recollection of any of it.

Hades ended the story with, "Your mother wasn't too happy about that. It was a delicate time. Lots of tension between Olympians."

"Isn't that always the case?" Hip pointed out.

"Right you are," Hermes said. "Except for times like these when we share a common enemy."

"Any theories about who's behind this?" Hip asked.

"None yet. You?"

Hip shook his head. He didn't have a clue, which wasn't the best start to a quest with so much riding on it.

Therese hadn't felt this nervous since the day she stood on the platform in Circe's battlefield preparing to face the monsters while Jen and Marvin held her babies in the cave where she'd given birth to them. She and Than had stayed up late last night talking, and they had decided it was time to tell Carol and Richard the truth.

Therese thought it would be better if she told them alone, so, while Than took the twins and Lynn for a swim in Lemon Reservoir across the street, Therese sat down in her childhood living room on a chair across from her aunt and uncle and took a deep breath.

"Is everything okay?" Carol asked.

"We're here for you no matter what," Richard said. "Just calm down and tell us what's on your mind."

Therese took another deep breath and let it out slowly, trying not to let her teeth chatter. She'd kept this secret from them for so long—for over five years. She wasn't just afraid of their reaction to the fact that Than had been the god of death and that her children were demigods; she was also afraid that they'd be hurt that she hadn't confessed it all sooner.

"This may come as a shock to you," Therese began.

<u>CHAPTER TWELVE</u>

A Giant Strikes Again

By the time Hypnos saw the enormous serpent's tail whipping down at him from above the canyon, it was too late to do anything about it. Like a fly, he was swatted against the hard canyon floor, crushed. He immediately reintegrated to heal, leaving the other gods on the hunt. They prayed to him with questions—was he okay, had he been attacked, what was his location—but his brain was spinning, spinning, spinning, and he couldn't reply.

When he could see again, the beast was above him, straddling the canyon as it had done to Ares. Hip tried with all his might to put the beast into the deep boon of sleep, but when that failed, he leapt to his feet and conjured his sword. He would not let this Giant win.

As he was about to tell the others where he thought he was, one of the Giant's heads opened its ferocious jaws and spit fire at him, singeing Hip's hair and skin. He spun around, putting out the flames and creating a current to protect himself, but then a second head bore down on him, its tongue lashing against him. Hip drove his sword through the roof of the creature's mouth. The tip of his blade cut clean through and stuck up from the beast's snout like the horn of a rhino. The monster screeched and wailed and thrashed, lifting its head in the air. When it did, Hip felt the agonizing pain of teeth crunching through his bones and of the arm holding his sword being severed from his body. Like the beast, he screamed in pain.

In the next instant, a god whom Hip had never before seen leapt on-to the impaled head of the beast. The god had long white hair and a white beard and chrome-colored eyes. His skin was pale and his face beautiful as he sat on the beast's head and clamped its jaw shut with his legs. Even though he was in agonizing pain, with blood pouring from his body, Hip distracted the other two heads while the other god used his entire body to brace open the jaws of the third. In one quick motion, the stranger snatched the arm and the sword from the beast. Then, holding Hip's arm in one hand and the sword in the other, the white god gouged out both eyes on the Giant's head, before flipping around in the air like a frantic bee.

Hip watched on with amazement as the stranger gouged out the oth-er four eyes on the Giant with lightning speed. Then he beckoned Hip to follow him, and, since the god had his arm, Hip followed.

Than stood at the door of the twins' bedroom watching Therese reading a bedtime a story. She sat on a bean bag chair between the two beds, where Hermie and Hestie lay curled beneath their blankets, listening. They did not look the least bit sleepy, even though he'd spent three hours playing with them and Therese's sister, Lynn, in the lake before supper. Instead, they giggled at the funny parts and spoke out loud the parts they knew.

When the story ended, Than stepped into the room to kiss each of his children on the forehead and wish them a goodnight. "Say hello to your Uncle Hip for me," he added.

Therese bent over them and did the same, giving Clifford a kiss as well. He was curled up next to Hestie, because tonight it was her turn to sleep with him.

Then he and Therese closed the kids' bedroom door and headed downstairs toward their own.

As they changed out of their clothes into something more comfortable, Than asked, "How did it go today with Carol and Richard? Could they accept the truth?"

Therese pulled her favorite nightshirt over her head and said, "Not at first. They thought I was playing a joke on them."

"That's to be expected." He pulled back the covers from their unmade bed and climbed beneath them.

Therese took a brush to her hair. "When I told them it wasn't a joke, they thought I had lost my mind. I had to call Mrs. Holt—I mean Mrs. Stern—and Bobby to come over and vouch for me."

"It's too bad Jen couldn't be there to demonstrate," Than said.

"I prayed to her to come, but I never heard back."

"I'm sure she's busy. You know how it is."

Therese frowned and put down the hairbrush. "Yeah." Then she crawled into bed beside him.

"I bet they had a lot of questions. I wish I could have been there to help answer them."

"No. It was better that I went alone."

"You really think so?"

"I wasn't sure how they'd react to the idea that you were once Death." She caressed his cheek. "I didn't want you to see the horror on their faces."

"It wouldn't have been the first time someone reacted that way. I'm a big boy, Therese. I should have been there."

"Then what would we have done with the kids? I didn't want them to be confused or to feel like Carol and Richard couldn't accept us all for how we are."

"Do they accept it, or not?"

"It's going to take some time." She put her hand on his chest.

His heartbeat sped up at her touch. He put his left arm around her—the one that wasn't in a cast—and pulled her close to him. "How were they when you left them?"

"They weren't angry at me, at least."

"Why would they have been angry at you?"

"Um, for lying to them for five years?"

"You did it to protect them."

"That's what I told them. I explained about what had happened to Pete and told them that's why the Holts know. I also told them that Mr. Stern doesn't know, and that they need to protect Mrs. Stern's secret."

"Did you tell them about your parents?" he asked.

She looked up at him and shook her head. "I was afraid that would be too much to swallow, you know? Maybe it's best I tell them everything in bite-size pieces."

"Maybe you're right." He gave her a soft, reassuring kiss. Then he asked, "Was there anything else you didn't tell them?"

"I left out a lot of things," she said. "I didn't tell them about the Maenads, for one. That would really freak them out. I didn't tell them about how you made me a god by smearing me with ambrosia and setting us both on fire. I also didn't tell them about Carol's role in my parents' murder. I left out McAdams and Ares and all of that. I just said we met while I was in the coma. I didn't tell them about how I fought McAdams in Circe's battlefield, or how I went through Hades's challenges. I *did* tell them I was the goddess of animal companions, though. And I told them about Hermie and Hestie having an important destiny—which is why we became mortal."

"Bite-size pieces," he said before kissing her again. "That's a smart idea."

When he looked down at her again, he saw her frowning.

"What is it?" he asked. "Do you regret saying anything to them?"

"No. That's not it. It was actually a relief."

"Then what is it, honey?" He kissed each of her cheeks and stroked her hair. "Tell me what's bothering you."

Tears flooded her eyes and one dropped onto her cheek. He smoothed it away with his thumb.

"Honey?" he asked. "Tell me?"

"Talking about it with them today," she said. "It brought back so many amazing memories. I'm grateful for our incredible life together with our precious babies, and it's stupid, so stupid, to let those memories make me sad. I'm sorry. Just ignore me. Honestly, I'm pathetic."

He couldn't help but laugh at how hard she was on herself. "You silly goose," he said, borrowing a line Therese used on the kids. "You have every right to feel the way you do. It was a lot to give up."

"And even more for you. How can I complain when it must be so much harder for you?"

"Therese," he said as his own eyes unexpectedly filled with tears. "Don't you realize that I've never been happier? Being with you and our kids is more fulfilling than anything I ever experienced as a god."

She smiled up at him, her beautiful lips only inches from his. He closed the gap between them and showed her just how much he loved her.

Jen gasped from the lack of oxygen inside of Charybdis and strained her eyes to see. She realized the blindness couldn't be caused by lack of light, because, as a goddess, Jen could see in the dark and through objects. Her blindness had to be caused by the tight membrane closing all around her, like a cinched sack. She struggled against it, and when that got her nowhere, she remembered she could conjure a sword. She focused on the sword, as Hip had taught her, but the blade didn't come. She clenched her jaw tight and tried again, and this time, the hilt appeared in her hand.

She drove the blade through the membrane and was immediately accosted by bloody water. She blinked her eyes, spat, and wiped her face with her palms. The loud, thundering sound inside Charybdis was disorienting, yet she could see now that she was inside some kind of tube—like the monster's esophagus. She forced her way out into the swirling water inside the beast, and there, a few yards away, was Stormy! He floundered with his legs and neck against the whirlpool, and when he saw her, his eyes widened, and he tried with all his might to get to her.

She sheathed her sword at her waist and swam the fiercest breast-stroke of her life toward him. When she reached him, she wrapped her arms around his neck. Whatever happened now, they would endure it together.

CHAPTER THIRTEEN

The Stranger

Hip followed the stranger across the mountains of Greenland to the highest peak north of the Arctic Circle. The stranger entered a cave just below its summit. The entire area was covered in ice and snow.

But the cave itself was cozy and well stocked. There was an empty fireplace made of rock to the very back with a mantle where bowls and pots were stacked. Flanking the fireplace were a couch and a bed with a table between them. This was obviously the god's home.

"Come lie down," he said. "I can help you heal."

Hip went to the couch, keeping his hand on the shoulder where the arm had been severed. In spite of the pressure, blood seeped through his fingers and fell onto the rocky floor of the cave.

"We should call Apollo," Hip groaned as the god rubbed ice against the wound.

"We don't need him, Hypnos," the god said, just before he pressed the broken limb against Hip's shoulder. "This will hurt."

The god's hands became ablaze, like the sun. Hip clenched his jaw and resisted crying out. In a moment, the god's hands returned to normal. Hip looked down at his arm, panting for air. The blazing hands had cauterized his flesh, and the bleeding had stopped.

"The skin is attached," the god said, "but you need to hold still for several hours while the bone heals, too."

"Thanks." Hip relaxed against the back of the couch, feeling breathless and exhausted. "You know my name, but I don't believe we've met."

"No, we haven't," the god said. "I tend to keep to myself."

"Why did you help me, then?"

"You were in need of it." The god poured some wine into a golden goblet and handed it to Hip before pouring some for himself. "This is very old wine. It's good, no?"

It slid down smoothly and had the right mixture of dry and sweet. It tasted like the wine of Dionysus. "Very. Thank you."

The god shot a flame from his hand toward the log in the fireplace and set it ablaze. "That's better," he said. "Hungry?" He held out a bowl of peanuts.

Hip shook his head. "So, who are you?"

"If I tell you, you must swear on the River Styx to tell no one."

Hip furrowed his brow. "May I know why?"

"Like I said, I prefer to keep to myself. I'm a very old god who's been all but forgotten by the ruling pantheon, and I'd like to keep it that way."

Hip's curiosity won out. "I swear on the River Styx."

"My name's Aether."

Hip's head was still ringing from having been slammed against rock. "Did you say *Keeper*?" That was a strange name.

"Aether."

"Oh, I've heard of you," Hip said. "You're the god of the upper air."

The god took another sip of his wine. "I'm surprised you've heard of me. I don't even figure into any of the creation stories anymore."

"You came from Chaos and formed the heavenly stars, right?"

The white god nodded. "I am the air that the Olympians breathe, though they know very little of me."

"Because you prefer to keep to yourself?"

"That's right." He finished the last of his wine and refilled it from the bottle on the table. "More?"

"No, thanks, I'm good." Then he added, "I can't thank you enough for what you did today."

"You can thank me by keeping me out of the stories that you tell to the other gods."

"We could use your help," Hip said. "Someone has been attacking Gaia and releasing Giants, like the one we fought today. That monster swallowed Ares's leg, and we need to get it back."

"I have an herb you could leave by the beast while he sleeps. If he eats it—and he most likely will—it will cause him to regurgitate the contents of his stomach. Then you can wait for the Giant to move on before you go back for the leg. That way, you wouldn't have to fight him again."

Hip grinned. "Dude, you're my new best friend."

A prayer from Persephone made Hip frown. *Where are you?*

Jen held on to Stormy's neck as the whirlpool pushed them around.

"I'm so sorry I got us into this," she said to Stormy. "Will you ever forgive me?"

He whinnied a reply that she understood as, "I already have."

In the next moment, they were thrust from the round, menacing, suckermouth of Charybdis onto hard sand. Jen spat out water as she jumped to her feet. Then she helped Stormy up as Charybdis receded back into the sea. On the shore beside them were Keto and Scylla, and they were smiling.

Jen looked around. They were on a small island the size of her barn back home. The question was, which island?

"Where are we?" she asked, panting.

Keto laughed. "If I wanted you to know that, I wouldn't have had Charybdis swallow you up and bring you here."

Jen met Scylla's gaze. "What are you going to do now?"

"Teach you a lesson," Scylla said. "No one is disrespectful to my mother without consequences. She was once the queen of the seven seas. And one day she may be again."

Jen narrowed her eyes at Keto. "Do you have something to do with the attacks on Gaia?"

Keto shrugged. "Your people already questioned me. I'm sorry to say I can't take credit for that."

Keto's reference to the Olympians as *Jen's people* lifted Jen's confidence. It had been a year since she'd joined them as a goddess, and she was still getting used to the idea. "But you know who's behind it?"

"I didn't at the time I was questioned," she said.

"And now?"

"I don't think I want to divulge that to you," Keto said. "Even if I *am* sending you to a place where you'll never be able to tell anyone anyway."

"Which is?"

"My husband's hungry stomach," Keto said. "He's *always* hungry. And he's *irritable* when he's hungry. And, for some reason, he thinks it's *my duty* to feed him. If I slip you down his throat whole, you'll make his stomach feel full, and I'll get that crabby merman off my back for good."

Jen's knees trembled. She felt like she was going to collapse onto the sand. Should she pray for help and risk getting Stormy eaten, too? Or could she figure out how to get them both out of this mess on her own? She glanced around the island again, trying to come up with a plan. She needed to find a way to stall these monsters so she could think of something. Maybe she would draw her sword and take her chances.

"Your husband doesn't sound like a very nice guy," Jen said, grasping at straws.

"He was once the King of the Sea," Scylla said. "So you need to be more respectful."

"Do you know what they call him *now*?" Keto asked. "The Old Man of the Sea. Do you know how insulting it is for a *deity* to be called an *old man*? It's demeaning."

"If you want more respect from the Olympians," Jen said, "why are you always threatening them? Why not work with them, become allies, and earn their respect?"

Jen could tell by Keto's ever reddening complexion that she had said the wrong thing.

The merwoman darted across the sand and shouted angrily in Jen's face, "I don't need to earn anything from anyone! I'm already owed it because of who I am. I am the mother of all monsters, and there is no one who should be more greatly feared than I!"

Jen shrank back, her heart pounding against her throat, her throat closing up. "You promised you would let Stormy go. I've cooperated. Now set him free."

"Not until you're in my husband's stomach!"

Hip winced at the pain in his shoulder as he took another sip of the wine and studied his host. He wondered why Aether was so bent on keeping to himself. Was there more to his story? He recalled being told that the ancient god had sided with the Olympians during their war with the Titans by creating a shield over Tartarus that had helped keep the enemies down; but, beyond that, Hip knew nothing of him. Hip thought later he might ask his cousin Aeolus—that windbag—what he knew, since it was likely the two deities had crossed paths from time to time. For now, he told his mother he was okay but injured. But then she asked about Jen, saying that Hecate had been summoned to the duties of Sleep.

"Are you sure you don't want more?" Aether asked of the wine.

As Hip was about to reply to his mother, he received an urgent prayer from Jen. "Oh no." He sat up on the couch and winced with pain.

"What is it?" Aether asked.

Hip felt the blood leave his face. "My wife is about to be swallowed by Phorcys."

"Where are they?" Aether asked.

"On a tiny island. That's all she knows."

"I have an idea where," Aether said, getting to his feet. "If you swear to say nothing about me to the other gods, I'll guarantee her safety."

"How can you guarantee it?" Hip asked, on the verge of praying to his father.

"If I can't save her before she's swallowed, I'll use my herb to get her out."

"Her horse, too," Hip said.

"I'll be back soon." Aether hovered at the mouth of the cave. "And remember, no one is to know my name."

In his desperation, Hip agreed, but he felt uneasy about the god's demand.

Than went over the safety rules with the passengers on his raft where they were docked near the bank of the Animas River just before nine in the morning. He had three little ones and their parents aboard today, which wasn't uncommon, since he always guided the two-hour tours. The more experienced guides preferred the longer, all day trips, and Than didn't want to be away from his family for that long. Besides, with his arm still healing, the easy, two-hour tours were all he could handle.

The three little black-haired boys probably ranged in age between seven and ten. Their little faces peered up at him from over their orange life vests. The two younger boys were full of smiles, but the oldest gripped his vest with white knuckles. His face was paler than that of his brothers.

"We're going to take it slow at first," Than explained. "If you want me to speed things up or make the ride more thrilling for you, just let me know."

"I wanna go fast!" the youngest said.

The oldest boy frowned. "But not too fast. Safety first."

"Smart boy," Than said to the oldest. "Safety will always be our priority."

The oldest boy forced a smile and then asked, "Are you sure you can do this with that arm in a cast?"

"Absolutely," Than assured him. "I can use my hand. The cast is just there to make sure my elbow heals in place."

The boy didn't seem too convinced.

Than added, "And if anyone wants me to stop the raft at any time, just speak up."

Than untied the raft from the dock and pushed them off. He sensed the fear in the oldest boy, noticed the shiver that traveled down his spine. To make him feel less afraid and to distract him from his worries, Than made conversation. He asked where the family was from, how long they were staying, what else were they doing while they were in Colorado (they were from Arizona), and what did they think of Colorado so far. Than helped them spot Rocky Mountain bighorn sheep, moose, rabbits, and other wildlife along the mountains on either side of them as they made their way through the narrow gorge.

Than relished the presence of these living souls. Never in his ancient life could he had ever predicted that he would one day have this chance to board joyous mortals, full of life and wonder, nor could he have anticipated the breathtaking ride over the river he'd offer them day after day. If Charon knew, would he be green with envy?

In spite of the conversation, Than took in the amazing views, unable to believe that the season was already coming to an end. He had taken the job in May, which didn't seem that long ago, and now here he was, guiding the last ride of the year. By mid-September, the weather became too cold and the rivers too slow for the trips to be safe and enjoyable for most people. In June, the snow melting from the mountains reinvigorated the river and easily trimmed what was a two-hour tour in September by thirty minutes.

As much as he would miss the breathtaking views and the exhilarating ride down the river, Than was having a hard time relating to the melancholy Therese had been feeling lately. She missed being a goddess far more than he missed being a god. Maybe it was because he had been one for centuries longer, or maybe it was because his job as Death had been monotonous. Maybe it was because he was still reeling in the incredible sensations a mortal body experienced—which was profoundly more intense than what a god experienced of the world.

He was enjoying his life as a husband and a father in the Upperworld. He loved the Colorado mountains, the trees, the birds, and the raging river. He especially enjoyed sharing these things with the twins.

But he did miss his immortal family. He'd forgotten how frequently he used to communicate with his brother and sisters, even if they didn't see each other face-to-face as often as they'd liked. And although his father wasn't a big talker, his mother used to make a point of speaking to him regularly.

Since becoming a mortal, Than prayed to them on a regular basis, but he was never sure if they actually heard his prayers.

Jen gave Stormy a frightful look of apology as she stood on the bank of the tiny island where Charybdis had delivered them. Phorcys appeared, looking put out about having to travel away from his dilapidated castle.

"What's this all about?" he asked Keto and Scylla from the shallow water lapping at the bright, warm sand.

"Suppertime," Keto said.

The Old Man of the Sea glanced first at Jen and then back at his wife. "You foolish woman!" Phorcys growled. "This goddess is a favorite of Hades. Do you think it wise to incur his wrath?"

"That's not going to happen," Scylla replied. "Hades will never know."

"We forced her to cooperate," Keto explained, "by threatening the life of her beloved horse."

"I'd rather eat the beast than the girl," Phorcys said.

"No!" Jen cried. "They promised to spare him!"

At that moment, the oxygen seemed to thin, as it had in the belly of Charybdis. Jen looked at the others, and all of them, even Stormy, were gasping for air like fish out of water. Keto and Phorcys flung themselves out to sea, but Scylla and Jen merely stared at one another with wide eyes as Stormy fell on the bank and they were left weak, barely able to stand, gasping at air, where none came.

Just as Jen fell to the sand and closed her eyes, she felt something whisk her up from the ground and carry her off. She opened her mouth wide, but still no air came, so she stopped straining and gave into the nothingness that wanted her.

CHAPTER FOURTEEN

Tracks and Tricks

Jen gasped for air and opened her eyes to brightness and clouds. Stormy was scrambling to his feet beside her. The two of them were alone outside the gates of Mount Olympus.

"How did we get here, boy?"

He whinnied an "I don't know."

"Well, that's strange." She checked her body, and, finding it intact, added, "Someone saved us. I wonder who?"

Just then the clouds on which they were standing trembled at the arrival of Swift and Sure, the black stallions belonging to Hades. The stallions pulled the chariot behind them, and when they came to an abrupt stop, Hades peered down at Jen from behind the reins and asked, "What are you doing here?"

"I'm not sure," she said. And then she told him what had happened, even though it meant admitting that she'd been wrong about Scylla.

He glanced behind him. "And you have no idea who or what brought you here?"

"None at all."

Before Hades could question her further, the gates of Mount Olympus opened, and Persephone rushed into her husband's arms.

"Oh, I've missed you!" Persephone cried as she covered Hades's face with her kisses.

Hades kissed her tenderly, but then pulled away, cleared his throat, and said, "We have an audience."

With a bag hanging from each shoulder, Hecate lingered at the gate, accompanied by Cubie and Galen, but Jen had a feeling Hades was referring to *her* and not to Persephone's entourage.

"Thank goodness you're all right," Persephone said to Jen. "When the duties of Sleep summoned Hecate, we didn't know what to think."

"What?" Jen asked with surprise. Aloud, she cried out in a desperate prayer, "Hip!"

When Hip heard Jen's frantic prayer, he assured her that he was okay. And when he discovered that she and Stormy were safe, he sat back on Aether's couch overcome with relief. The duties of Sleep had still not called to him, but he knew it wouldn't be long, and then he would fly straight to her and hold her in his arms.

Tell me where you are, she prayed. *Stormy and I will come right away.*

You need to rest, Hip replied. *And this region is too dangerous. It won't be much longer. I promise.* Then he asked, *How's Muggie?*

He's with Hecate. I'm going to him now. His conversation with Jen was cut short when Aether returned to the cave, bringing with him a glow that illuminated the room.

Before the god had even sat down, Hip said, "Thank you for saving Jen."

"Remember your promise," the god said.

"Of course."

"As soon as you feel up to it, I'll show you how to track the beast." Aether sat on the bed across from Hip and finished the last of the wine in his cup. "Then we'll leave the herb for him and wait."

Hip wondered if the god expected something in return. "Why are you helping me?"

"Because you need it."

Therese had just put the twins down for their afternoon nap when, as she came down the stairs, she caught a glimpse of Than through their bedroom door. Both of his arms were over his head—the arm in the cast bent like the letter "L." He was trying to get into his gray t-shirt. He'd managed to get into his jeans, though they hadn't yet been buttoned. But the shirt was giving him trouble. Therese should have rushed to his side to help him, but, instead, she stood there and watched, taking in the view of her husband. He didn't have to be a god to have the body of one. He might not have super strength and super speed, but, boy oh boy, did he have super form.

"I can hear you breathing," he said. "Are you just going to stand there, or are you going to help me."

She laughed but stayed where she was. "So, you can guide a raft careening down the Animus River for two hours with the safety of people's lives in your hands, but you can't put on a shirt?"

"Very funny. I'm tired of wearing button-downs. I miss my soft t-shirts."

"Poor baby," she teased as she finally went to his aid. But before she pulled the shirt down, she kissed his bare chest and abs, all the way down to his belly button.

He gasped. "Oh, my."

The sound of a throat being cleared made the hair on the back of Therese's neck stand up. She turned toward the door to see Persephone watching them from the hallway.

"Hello," the goddess said with cheeks as red as Therese's must have been.

"Mother?" Than was still hidden inside the shirt.

Therese pulled it down for him.

"This is awkward," he muttered.

"Aren't you glad to see me?" Persephone asked.

"Of course." He crossed the room and kissed her.

Therese followed him and did the same. That's when she noticed Jen in the living room sitting on the couch with Muggie.

"We hope we haven't come at a bad time," Persephone added.

"We just put the twins down for their nap," Therese said. "But they usually don't sleep for more than an hour. Can you stay that long?"

"I may need to, anyway," Persephone said. "I have something very important to discuss with you. We better sit down."

Hip lay back on Aether's couch drinking down the last sip of his third cup of wine when he felt the duties of Sleep call to him. This meant his body was healed, and he was ready to go. The first thing he did, after disintegrating and dispatching directly to the Fields of Asphodel to relieve Hecate, was to look for Jen and Muggie. He was disappointed to learn that they were visiting Than and Therese. Unless he wanted to put the mortals into the deep boon of sleep, he'd have to wait a while longer to see his family.

Great. He already thought of Muggie as part of his family. That was probably not a good thing.

Aether seemed anxious to get started tracking the Giant, so after the god snubbed out the fire in the fireplace, the two set out above the cold mountains of Greenland.

Hip followed as Aether hovered above a canyon.

"This is where I found you," Aether said. "We can track him from here."

"But the snow has covered any tracks the beast may have left behind," Hip pointed out.

"We don't need the tracks."

"Then what?"

"Gravity and magnetism," Aether said.

Hip scratched at his chin. "Huh?"

Aether beckoned Hip to follow him as he flew over the mountains of Greenland. "The Giants were born of Gaia, and their bones, teeth, and scales are made of dense iron."

"No wonder." Hip rubbed at his shoulder, recalling the sharp pain he'd felt when the beast's teeth had cut through Hip's bone.

"So you see, I can detect a subtle difference in the gravitational pull of the earth when I'm flying over very dense objects. I can also sense a change in magnetism the closer I get to them."

Hip hadn't expected a science lesson. "How do you know all this? I fly around the globe all day, every day, and I didn't know that."

"You're always focused on the mortals. All I do is refresh the air for the gods and occasionally adjust the brightness of the heavenly stars. I have nothing else to do, so I notice these things."

"Fair enough," Hip muttered.

"Unfortunately, if we fly too quickly, we could miss the change."

They spent the day flying across Greenland, and when the light from Helios dipped to the west and Selene made her way from the south, Hip and Aether crossed the Baffin Bay to investigate the mountains of northern Canada. Aether said he felt a subtle change in magnetism in that direction.

Soon they were enveloped by the magical lights of the aurora borealis—also known as the northern lights. The pink, green, purple, blue, and yellow hues were breathtaking.

"Do you feel that?" Aether asked.

"You mean the northern lights?"

"No," the god said. "The change in gravity. I think we've found our beast."

Therese served Muggie a bowl of raviolis and a cup of lemonade while Persephone and Than caught up on what each had been doing since their last visit. When Muggie had finished, Therese offered him some oatmeal cookies, which he ate on the living room floor while he played with Legos and blocks.

When Therese joined Than on the couch, where he sat beside his mother, Persephone turned to Jen, who'd taken the rocking chair, and said, "Tell them about the deal Hypnos has made with Zeus."

Jen's face reddened. "The boy doesn't know. And he's getting better at understanding regular English."

Muggie looked up from where he was playing and said something Therese couldn't understand. She got the, "Me, tannie?" but that was it.

Jen stammered. "Um, what your favorite color is. Remember? I asked you, and you didn't know."

He nodded. "Ja, nee. I like dem all." Then he went back to the toys.

Therese met Jen's smile of relief with her own. "Maybe you can speak in general terms?"

Than stood up. "Just tell me if my brother's okay."

"For now." Persephone took Than's wrist and pulled him back down on the couch beside her.

Than leaned toward his mother. "What does that mean?"

"Hip wants to have a k-i-d," Jen said.

"But that's impossible," Therese pointed out.

"That's what we thought, too," Persephone explained. "But Zeus and Hera and Aphrodite and the others are all anxious to get Ares's leg back."

"What?" Than glanced at Therese with wide eyes before turning to face his mother. "What's going on?"

Therese and Than held hands as they listened to Persephone and Jen explain what had happened to Ares. As much as Therese resented Ares for being responsible for her parents' deaths, she was also grateful to him for saving Hermie's life during their fight with the monsters in Circe's battlefield. And even if he hadn't saved her child, she didn't really want him to go through eternity without his leg, especially for Aphrodite's sake.

"Aphrodite must be beside herself," Therese murmured.

"Hip agreed to use his power of disintegration to find the Giant," Persephone went on. "He said he would bring back Ares's leg and find out who's releasing the monsters in exchange for what Jen has already mentioned."

"Where is he now?" Than asked.

"He was hurt," Jen said, "but he's okay."

"You've seen him?" Persephone asked.

Jen shook her head. "He just regained his power of disintegration. He didn't want to put all the mortals to sleep."

"I bet you're anxious to go," Therese said.

"Very. No offense. Now that Muggie's fed, do you mind if we take off?" Jen asked Persephone.

"Go have your reunion," Persephone said. "Because then I want mine."

Jen gave everyone a hug and asked Muggie to say thank you and goodbye.

"What about my friends, tannie?" Muggie asked.

"They're still sleeping," Jen replied. "We'll come back tomorrow." She turned to Therese. "Is that okay?"

"Do you seriously have to ask?" Therese teased.

After Jen had god-traveled back to the Underworld with Muggie, Persephone cleared her throat and said, "There's an important reason why I wanted to talk to you about Hypnos."

"You mean other than the fact that he's my brother, and I should know when he's in danger?" Than asked, a bit sarcastically.

Persephone put a hand on her son's shoulder. "I'm sorry we don't keep you better informed. We don't want to worry you when there's so little you can do about it."

Therese doubted Persephone's reply had made Than feel any better. "What's the other reason?"

"I don't want to get your hopes up too high, my darlings," Persephone said with a huge smile on her face. "But if Zeus is willing to make this deal with Hypnos, then what's preventing him from making a similar deal with you?"

Therese and Than exchanged looks of confusion.

"What are you saying?" Than asked.

"If Hypnos succeeds in his quest and that boy becomes like us…"

"What do you mean 'that boy'?" Therese asked. "You mean Muggie? Hip and Jen want to adopt Muggie and make him their child?"

"Yes." Persephone tucked a strand of her blonde hair behind her ear.

"Wow," Therese whispered. "Jen always said she never wanted kids of her own."

"As you know, people change," Persephone said.

"So, what kind of deal would we make with Zeus?" Than asked. "Our children have to be *here*, in the Upperworld, in order to fulfill their destinies."

"We would never abandon them," Therese added.

"That's not at all what I'm suggesting," Persephone said. "But once they've fulfilled their destinies, what's to prevent you from making a similar deal to have immortality restored to all four of you?"

Therese held her breath and sat very still. Had she heard Persephone correctly?

Than shook his head. "But the Fates are never wrong."

"They said you would have two children," Persephone recited. "But none immortal."

"Exactly," Than said. "So what you're saying is impossible, according to the Fates."

"Not necessarily," Persephone said with a mischievous smile.

C H A P T E R   F I F T E E N

Reunions

While Hip managed the dreams of the mortals and followed Selene around the dark side of the earth, bringing slumber to those who needed it, he also hovered with Aether above the Canadian Rockies, waiting for the Giant to eat the herb that would make him cough up Ares's leg.

The Giant was still blind from having his eyes gouged out. Hip had no idea if the blindness was permanent; nevertheless, the beast's acute sense of hearing and of smell more than made up for it. The Giant knew he wasn't alone, as his aggressive stance clearly demonstrated, but if Hip and Aether didn't see where the leg was regurgitated, they might not ever find it. Unlike the Giant, who could be tracked by Aether, using gravity and magnetism, the leg could perish in the ice and eventually be unsalvageable.

Hip's impatience with the Giant vanished the moment Jen and Muggie entered the Fields of Asphodel and embraced him. Muggie instantly fell asleep in his arms. He kissed the boy's cheek and lay him in the flowers, in the warm spot, on which Hip had just been lying himself. Then he turned his full attention to Jen.

"You certainly know how to make life interesting," he said to her.

"Don't give me a hard time about it, Hip." She threw her arms around his neck. "Just kiss me and tell me you forgive me."

He pressed his mouth to hers—harder than he had intended. She responded by taking his hair in her fists and pulling him down into the flowers beside the sleeping child.

Back at the Canadian Rockies, Aether said something to Hip telepathically.

What did you say? Hip asked the white god of the upper air.

I said he's eating the herb.

But Hip had long forgotten about the herb and the Giant and Ares's leg. The only thing he cared about at the moment was Jen, holding Jen, loving Jen.

Than helped Therese cook supper while Persephone and the twins sat around the kitchen table molding clay into figures. He was pleased to see Hestie make a three-headed dog that was meant to be Cerberus, and, when Than asked Hermie what he was making, the boy said, "Grampa Hades."

"What about me?" Persephone asked them.

"You're next!" Hermie assured her.

Persephone kissed the boy on the cheek. "I wish I could stay longer to see you make it, but I really must go."

Just then, the back door burst open, and Carol entered the kitchen. Her eyes were red-rimmed, and she was trembling. She immediately noticed Persephone at the kitchen table and said, "I'm sorry. I should have called. I didn't know you had company."

"Carol, what's wrong?" Therese wiped her hands on a dish towel and crossed the room to her aunt. "You've been crying."

"I'll talk to you about it later," she said. "When you don't have guests." She glanced again at Persephone. "Isn't this Than's mother?" Carol's eyes widened. "Wait! Isn't she…" Carol's voice trailed off. Her face became as white as the kitchen sink.

Persephone stood from the table and shook Carol's hand. "It's lovely to see you again. I see you finally know who I am."

Carol stared back at her blankly.

"I'm afraid I was just leaving," Persephone said.

The goddess kissed each of the twins, blew kisses to Than and Therese, and then disappeared.

Carol collapsed onto a kitchen chair, apparently struggling to breathe.

"Carol?" Than asked.

Therese took Carol's hand. "Can I get you some cold water?"

Carol nodded.

Therese brought her a glass full of ice and water. Than expected Carol to drink it, but instead, she splashed it into her own face and blinked several times, causing the twins to laugh. Then she looked around and asked, "So this isn't a dream?"

"Grammie?" Hestie laughed at the sight of Carol's hair plastered to her face. "Did you think you were in the Dreamworld with Uncle Hip?"

Hermie laughed, too.

Carol stared blankly at Hestie for a moment before she said, "That's exactly what I thought."

"What's brought you here all shaken up?" Therese asked.

"Steph called to ask if Richard could come down and help her and John and Bobby carry in a new sofa set they got in town."

"Did something happen?" Than asked.

Carol shook her head. "Before we hung up the phone, Steph asked if I'd learned to speak to your favorite red birds yet."

Than glanced at Therese, who met his gaze with a pale face.

Carol looked up at them and said, "So it's true, then? Are you telling me that the souls of your mother and father, of my sister and her husband, are in those two Cardinals?"

"Yes," Hermie said matter-of-factly, as he continued to work the clay with his fingers. "They talk to us all the time."

"They sing to the children," Therese explained.

"And they speak to us," Hestie said. "With words."

Therese and Than exchanged looks of shock.

Than knelt on the floor by the table between the kids so he could look at them at eye level. "This is serious, kids. Do you mean to say you can actually understand what the birds are saying to you?"

The kids looked at one another and nodded.

"We can understand all the animals," Hermie said. "Even Clifford."

Therese shouted for joy and jumped up and down before hugging everyone in the room. Clifford ran around the table, yapping his little bark.

Therese asked, "What's Clifford saying now?"

"He's so happy that you're happy," Hestie said.

Than felt warmth and joy wash over him as he continued to kneel between the twins and watch his happy wife.

"Do you know what this means?" Therese asked. "This means I can talk to them again, through the kids! I can communicate with my parents again!"

Than noticed that Carol was still pale and trembling where she sat at the table.

"Are you okay?" he asked her.

"No, but I will be."

Hermie held up the figure of clay he'd made. "This is my Grampa Hades."

"And this is his dog," Hestie added. "His name is Cerberus."

"Have you met them?" Carol asked, looking as though she was afraid of the answer.

"Of course," Hermie said. "We went to see them just last week."

Than was surprised when Carol's pale frown became a smile and she laughed hysterically. "Of course, you did! That's perfectly reasonable! You went to visit your grandparents in the *Underworld!*"

"Grandma Persephone wasn't there," Hermie corrected.

"She was still on Mount Olympus," Hestie explained.

"Of course, she was!" Carol laughed. "*Mount Olympus*! With the other gods and goddesses!"

"That's why she came today to see us," Hermie added.

Hestie nodded. "She's going back to the Underworld for the fall and winter while our great-grammie stays in her winter cabin. Right, Mommy?"

"That's right," Therese said.

"I may need another glass of ice water," Carol said.

Jen lay in the Asphodel between Muggie and Hip, with Hip's cheek against her heart. She played with his soft hair and listened to the gentle sound of his snores. She wished she could fall asleep, too. It had been weeks since she'd slept. But there was too much on her mind.

One thought swirling around in her head was her disappointment in herself for trusting Scylla when everyone had warned her not to. Jen had really believed that there was good in her.

And maybe there still was. Jen wasn't ready to give up on her completely.

But why? Why was she so desperate to believe that this monster could be rehabilitated? Jen had never been that kind of person before—the bleeding-heart who believed everyone was innately good. That was more Therese's style. No, Jen was usually less trusting, perhaps even to a fault. So why would she put herself and Stormy in danger? What was she trying to prove?

She supposed she might not ever figure out the answer to her question, and, as she was about to give up on it, another plagued her mind. Why was Hip tracking the Giant *alone*? He'd originally gone with half a dozen Olympians—until he lost his power of disintegration when he was hurt. He was healed now, so what was the deal? Why hadn't he rejoined forces with the others?

She kissed the soft hair on his head. "Hip? Will you disintegrate and meet me back in our rooms? I'm leaving Muggie here, though, with you, because I need to get back to my duties for a while."

He nodded without opening his eyes as she slipped out from beneath him, kissed him and Muggie once more, and then walked through the fields to their rooms.

Before she entered her abode, she heard shouting coming from the main palace. Curious, she turned down the winding corridor and followed the Phlegethon—the river of fire—to the back of Hades and Persephone's palace.

"I should have been consulted," she heard Hades shout. "This affects my domain."

"Our domain," Persephone corrected.

"Yes. Our domain."

"And how many centuries did you make decisions without consulting me? I didn't think you would object."

"I made those decisions long before the Athena Alliance gave us equal dominion over the Underworld, my dear, and it gives you no right to make decisions without me now."

"What would be the harm in having another deity among us?" Persephone asked. "Especially when he would bring joy to our son and his wife?"

"It's the principle of the matter," Hades pointed out. "Besides, I'm concerned less with another deity than I am with the well-being of Hypnos. We have no idea who's behind these attacks. Doesn't it bother you that he's in grave peril?"

"Of course, it bothers me, but the other gods said they would help him."

"And are they?"

"They were, until he was hurt. No one knew where he was for a while."

"Exactly my point."

"But he's fine now. He's back. He's already returned to his duties."

"A lucky break. And what happens the next time he's hurt by one of those beasts? What if we're not so lucky?"

A cold shiver worked its way down Jen's spine. Hades was right.

"Maybe you should have a word with him then, darling," Persephone said. "I don't want to fight with you. We've barely kissed since I've been home."

"Come here, my dear," Hades said. "I go crazy without you. Every year."

As Jen turned back to her rooms, Hecate appeared and said, "Hades is right, you know. Talk to Hypnos. Convince him that he should never work alone. We may lose him forever."

Jen's heart seemed to halt in her chest for a moment before she caught her breath and asked, "Did you have a vision?"

"Not a vision, but a bad feeling," she said. "If anyone can convince him to take these precautions, it's you. Good luck."

Hecate disappeared.

Jen entered her abode and found Hip waiting for her on their couch in front of the small stream of fire that ran alongside their den.

"What took you so long?" he asked.

She sat beside him and told him about the conversation she had overheard between his parents.

"They're right," she said. "You shouldn't be working alone."

"I'm being very careful. I promise."

"The other gods want to help. Persephone said that Athena is chomping at the bit to find you, but you haven't told her your location. Why?"

Hip frowned. "It's complicated."

"Don't give me that."

He took a deep breath and sighed. Telepathically, he said, *I'm not alone.*

Jen raised her brows. "You're not?"

I'm getting help from another god, but he's made me swear to tell no one his name. He likes to stay under the radar. He's only helping me because I need it.

"Wait a minute." Jen sat up and squared herself to him. "You got after me for trusting Scylla, and yet, without hesitation, you're trusting this god no one even knows about?"

"Sshh." *He's not unknown. He helped overthrow Cronos. He just likes to keep to himself.*

"But still…"

Hip ran his fingers through Jen's hair and pulled her lips to his. She kissed him back but then lifted her head. "I'm serious, Hip."

"He saved my arm, Jen. He saved you."

"What? You lost your arm?" She jumped from the couch and glared at him in shock. "Why didn't you tell me?"

"It's all good now. The dude was amazing the way he moved in and saved the day. I'm telling you, I can trust him."

Jen put her hands on her hips and squinted. "Why are you being so hardheaded? Why can't you just work with the gods we already know we can trust?"

He stood up and wrapped his arms around her waist. "You know what Ares did to Therese, right? You know what Athena did to Medusa. You know what Zeus did to Athena? How is trusting this lesser-known deity any riskier than trusting *them*?"

Jen pouted. "Then why the lecture about me trusting Scylla?"

"Scylla is a known enemy. This dude saved my arm and probably kept me—and definitely *you*—from being swallowed."

"Then take your sisters with you. Hecate. Your mother."

"Fine. If it'll make you feel better, I'll ask them." Hip lowered his voice. "I'm waiting for the Giant to cough up Ares's leg."

"What? How?"

"The other god has an herb that will make the beast vomit."

"That was actually pretty smart."

"See? This dude knows things."

"But that Giant isn't going to just stand there while you take the leg."

"Probably not." Hip smiled at her. "The other god will lure the Giant away."

"And then what?"

"I'll grab the leg and go to Mount Olympus."

Jen wrinkled her nose. "It sounds too easy. Things never work out the way you think."

"It sounds easy because it is. And don't worry. Before I leave again to find the one responsible for the attacks, I'll ask my sisters to go with me. Deal?"

Jen leaned in and kissed her husband's sweet lips. "Deal."

That night, Therese read to her children, tucked them in, and kissed them goodnight—including Clifford, who was in Hermie's bed this time. Then she headed downstairs with new feelings of exuberance and glee. It wasn't that she hadn't been happy all along. She loved her life in Colorado with her family and her part-time job at the animal shelter. She loved being a wife and mother and being close to her aunt and uncle and Lynn. But she'd been longing to fly through the sky, to god travel at the snap of a finger, to run and swim at super-fast speeds, to communicate freely with her parents, and to speak telepathically to Than and to the other gods. And, oh, how she missed living in the magnificence that was the Underworld. She missed the bats and the snakes and the river of fire. She missed her Underworld family, too. Most of all, she missed her ability to bring humans and their animal companions together with her bow and arrows.

There were still days when she reached for her bow and quiver before she remembered that they were gone. The day she became mortal again, they had disappeared. They had gone as quickly as they had appeared that day she had claimed her purpose on Mount Olympus.

And now, to be told by Persephone that there might be a chance for her to have it all again. Well, who could blame her for feeling giddy?

But Than didn't believe it. He'd said again and again that Persephone's idea seemed impossible. Even now, as she settled onto the couch beside him in front of the television, he noticed her expression of exuberance and frowned.

There was nothing he could say, though, to prevent her from having hope. Persephone had said that the words of the Fates would still ring true if the four of them were to one day undergo apotheosis—which was the process of a mortal being made immortal by Zeus with goblets of ambrosia on Mount Olympus. The Fates had said she and Than would *have* no immortal children, that they would *bear* no immortal children, and *that* had come to pass. But the Fates had *not* said that their mortal children wouldn't one day be transformed. Persephone seemed sure that if Therese and Than could think of something that Zeus desperately needed—if they found some kind of bargaining chip—then they could make the dream of reuniting with the gods a reality.

Than stroked her hair and met her smiling face. He kissed her gently and whispered, "Would you be unhappy living a mortal life with me and our children?"

Therese cupped his cheeks with both hands. "Of course not. I'm already happier than I ever thought possible."

As he kissed her again, she couldn't help but think that, although her words were true, Persephone had planted a seed of hope in Therese that could never be destroyed. Therese was determined to find a way to restore immortality to all four of them.

Hip groaned and pinched his nose at the mound of green and red slime that shot from the Giant's middle head and down the mountainside. Aether hovered in the sky beside him, apparently unaffected.

"That's so disgusting," Hip said. He covered his mouth and looked away. "Do you see the leg?"

"Not yet. Be patient."

Hip glanced back down at the beast in time to see the two outside heads spewing more slime. "Oh, gods."

"It's still better than fighting him. Wouldn't you agree?" Aether asked.

"Um, I'd say the jury's still out on that." He fought his own urge to vomit and was suddenly reminded of the time Hermes had fed him the Moly plant to protect Hip from Circe's dark magic.

That hadn't gone so well.

"There." Aether pointed to a patch of ice on a cliff edge. "See it?"

Hypnos narrowed his eyes. It was Ares's leg, all right, but it was covered in green and red slime. "Oh, boy. I don't suppose you know how to make it rain? Give the ol' leg a quick shower?"

"That's not my department," Aether said. "You'll want Iris for that—though, at this temperature and altitude, I have a feeling it would only turn into more ice and snow."

"Yeah, you're probably right. But thanks, man. Now all I have to do is figure out who let the dogs out in the first place. If I do that, Zeus will allow me to have a son."

"I didn't realize you had so much riding on this quest," Aether said.

"I'm afraid I've already invested quite a bit in the idea," Hip admitted.

"I'll go lure the Giant back toward the east. Once you've returned Ares's leg to Mount Olympus, come back, and I'll help you find the god responsible for this mess."

Hip frowned. "I promised my wife I'd work with my sisters. She doesn't like me working alone." Hip extended his hand to Aether, who shook it. "But thanks, man. I couldn't have gotten this far without you."

It was Aether's turn to frown. "That's too bad. I was beginning to enjoy your company."

"Same, my friend. Why don't you come out of hiding, back into the fold? Maybe you don't want to live under the radar after all."

"I wish I could, Hypnos, but I have my reasons. If you want to hear my story someday, you know where to find me. And if you don't make any progress with your sisters, feel free to come see me. I have a hunch about who's been attacking Gaia, but I can't risk saying so out here in the open. My cave is heavily warded. You're welcome anytime but come alone."

"Why didn't you tell me this earlier?" Hip asked.

"I didn't want to get involved," the god said. "But I've grown fond of you in this short time. I'd like you to have your son."

Before Hip could say more, the god flew down and taunted the Giant. Enraged, the beast leapt across the Canadian Rocky Mountains toward Aether, leaving Ares's leg behind.

Holding his breath to avoid the pungent odor, Hip cupped snow into his hands and melted it, using the water to rinse the leg until it was washed clean. He took up the leg and god traveled to Mount Olympus. At his request, the seasons opened the gates. Hip was alarmed when Hermes appeared near the whale fountain with a look of fright, shouting some kind of warning as he pointed at the gates. Hip dropped Ares's leg and turned.

Peering down at him just outside the still open gates was one of the heads of another Giant—one with eyes. It opened its iron jaws and spit fire as it filled the air with a terrifying shriek. The fire engulfing Hip strangely felt like ice, though it burned. When the flames gave way to smoke, Hip was lifted from Mount Olympus between iron teeth, and the slimy tongue of the monster forced him down its throat.

<u>CHAPTER SIXTEEN</u>

Rally

Jen was sitting beside Hip on their couch before the blazing Phlege-thon, stroking his cheek and enjoying his kisses, when, suddenly, he sat up, his eyes and mouth wide with terror.

"Hip?"

As he reached for her hand, he disappeared.

She jumped from the couch. "Hip!"

When he didn't reply—not even telepathically—she was overcome with panic. Unable to think, she ran from her rooms down the winding corridor toward the palace of Hades and Persephone. Before she reached their rooms, she felt the duties of Sleep take possession of her. She naturally disintegrated to the Fields of Asphodel, where Muggie was sitting up with a look of confusion on his face. She took him in her arms, held him close as he fell back to sleep, and cried her eyes out, muttering, "Don't you leave me here without you, Hypnos. Don't you dare leave me here without you!"

Back at the palace, she pounded on the door to Hades and Perseph-one's main chamber.

Hecate cracked open the door. "What's wrong?"

"It's Hip!" Jen cried.

Hecate swung the door open wide, and as Jen stepped inside, Hermes appeared.

"Where's Lord Hades?" he asked.

Hades entered from his bed chamber. "Here. What's happened?"

Persephone followed and clutched her husband's arm. Her face was twisted with worry. "Where's Hypnos?"

"He was taken…by a Giant at the gates of Mount Olympus," Hermes reported. "I saw it with my own eyes. I wasn't fast enough." Hermes looked like he was going to be sick.

"Taken where?" Hades asked.

"We don't know," Hermes replied. "We're assembling at Mount Olympus to organize a search party. You're wanted at once—and anyone else you can spare."

Hades raked a hand through his dark hair. "We'll take the chariot."

"One more thing," Hermes said. "I want you to give me permission to take over the duties of Death from Pete. We'll have more luck if one of us disintegrates all over the globe, and Pete doesn't have the level of experience yet. I plan to start straight away, while the rest of the Olympians organize themselves."

"Granted," Persephone said. Then she glanced at Hades, who nodded his agreement.

"Take me with you," Jen said to Hermes. "No one should go alone."

"Is that a good idea?" Persephone asked. "You're as inexperienced as your brother."

"I have no choice," Jen said. "I can't sit around and do nothing. I have to find Hip. I have to."

Hades crossed the room and pinched her chin affectionately. "Be careful. And never leave Hermes's side. Got it?"

She nodded as the blood rushed to her face. That was the first time Hip's father had ever touched her. Then she took Hermes's arm.

"Ready?" he asked her.

She'd forgotten that she wouldn't have Stormy. Whenever she took over the duties of Sleep for Hip, she disintegrated in invisibility mode all over the dark side of the earth—on foot—to bring slumber to the mortals. But she was positive that Hermes intended to fly. She would have to fly, too. She had no choice. Oh, gods! Her stomach twisted into a ball of knots.

"Jen?" Hecate asked. "Are you sure?"

Jen swallowed hard and nodded. "Let's go, Hermes."

Hip slid down the slimy tube that was the Giant's esophagus and landed into the red and green soup of its belly. Communicating telepathically from inside another being was nearly impossible, but he tried with all his might as he conjured a sword and sliced away at the beast's innards.

The Giant thrashed around, and Hip tumbled and sank into the bubbling slime. He was disgusted and battered. Maybe cutting his way out wasn't going to work. He sheathed his sword and flew up the esophagus, looking for an escape.

He was disgusted again when bits of something that was freshly killed came squirming down the monster's throat. Hip flew down to the belly, dodging the bloody bits as best he could. He wondered how his father had lived inside of Cronos's belly for so many years. Hip would rather sever his own head and exist in Tartarus without a body for all eternity than endure the foul pit that was the monster's stomach. But, for now, he wouldn't be too quick to give up.

Then suddenly the walls of the monster's belly contracted, forcing Hip and the other contents up the shoot. Pressed against him were the squirmy bits of what he now realized was a seal. Then the foul liquid engulfed him, and he closed his eyes. After a few minutes of extreme pressure, the throat opened, and Hip sailed through the air. His eyes were plastered shut, so he couldn't see where he was or where he was going. He rubbed at his eyes just as his body bashed against solid rock and knocked him out.

While Jen stood beside Hades, Persephone, and the Furies in the great hall of the gods on Mount Olympus, where Zeus and the others were discussing a plan to set traps for the Giants and, hopefully, rescue Hip, she was also clinging to Hermes's arm as they flew over many parts of the world all at once.

Hermes patted her hand, which gripped his upper arm like a vice. "You know I like you, Jen. I really do. And I know you're worried for Hip—I am, too. But can I have just a little breathing room?"

She felt the blood leave her face. "You remember that problem I had the last time I tried to play Night Frisbee?"

Hermes's mouth dropped open. "No. You aren't serious, are you? You still can't fly?"

Jen averted her eyes, scanning the land below for signs of Hip.

"You should have stayed back, then," he said. "I'm better off without you."

"No. Please. My heart is aching." Tears fell on her cheeks just before the wind carried them away.

He rolled his eyes. "Don't cry."

She sniffed. "Sorry."

"You do know that even if you fall on your arse, you'll recover, right? So there's nothing to fear, really."

"There's the pain."

"Actually, haven't you noticed that your sense of touch is less— what's the word I'm looking for…"

"Refined?"

"Yes," he said. "Gods can see and hear better than mortals, there's no doubt about that. But we can't taste and feel as richly, I don't think. So the pain isn't as profound, and it never lasts."

"I guess that makes sense." She continued to watch below for signs of Hip. "It's not the pain that terrifies me, Hermes. I'm a pretty tough girl and have taken my fair share of pain. No, that's not what's holding me back."

"Then what?"

She looked at him sideways. "I'm terrified of losing control of myself, of flailing about like an idiot. I can't stand the feeling of not being in control of my own body. Maybe that's why I never learned to skate or to ski."

"But you learned to swim. It's the same thing."

"Therese has said that, too, but it's not. Water presses back. Air is…" she swept her free hand around, "it's nothing. There's nothing to hold onto, no leverage, no traction to keep me from flopping all over the place."

"There is, too, pressure and traction in air," Hermes said. "You just have to feel for it."

"I've tried, Hermes. Believe me. And I look like the biggest idiot, just spiraling out of control."

"Why do you spiral? Why do you even move your arms at all?"

"Therese told me to swim the breaststroke. I end up flipping around and making myself dizzy until I just lose control and fall toward the sea—I only ever practice over water."

He stopped over the Gulf of Mexico. In other parts of the world, they continued to search, especially over the mountains in the upper half of the northern hemisphere. But over the Gulf of Mexico, Hermes took both of her hands and said, "Don't swim the breaststroke. Instead, think about pushing off the ground with your toes."

"Really?' She looked back at him skeptically.

"Look. If I could teach Therese and Than how to drive, I sure as hell can teach you how to fly."

She giggled nervously.

"Go on," he said. "Try it."

She pointed her toes hard toward the sea, flailed, and fell against Hermes's chest, exactly the kind of thing she'd been afraid of. As he helped her upright, her face burned.

"Not so hard," he said. "Pretend you're gently reaching up on your toes to give me a kiss."

Jen didn't think her face could get any hotter.

"A friendly peck on the cheek," he added. "From one cousin to another."

She smiled. "Okay."

Very softly and slowly, she pressed down with her toes. Although she was still holding onto both of Hermes's hands, she glided above him, her head above his.

He looked up at her and nodded. "Very good."

She pulled on his hands until their shoulders were level—though whether he came up or she went down, she wasn't sure. "Let me try that again."

She pushed with her toes and glided upward. She felt like Charlie in the Chocolate Factory, experimenting with the fizzy lifting drink.

"Are you ready to try without holding onto me?" he asked her.

"Stay close, okay?"

"Promise."

She let go of his hands and pushed down with her toes. Although she wobbled a little from side to side, she held out her arms and regained her balance, pressing with her toes to keep herself upright.

"That's it," Hermes said. "Just practice hovering in one place. Learn to feel the air pressing back. Feel it?"

It helped when the wind blew. In between currents, she lost a bit of altitude, but not enough to make her lose control and scream, like she had so many other times. The idea of pressing down with her toes resonated with her. She pressed down with her palms in a similar way.

But up was the only direction she could go. She still couldn't maneuver forward through the air. She wouldn't be of any use to the other gods until she mastered that.

She continued to hover over the Gulf of Mexico, but in other parts of the world, she clung to Hermes's arm and scanned the earth like a hawk.

"See anything?" he asked her again.

"I see lots of things. But no Giants, yet."

"Hold on," he said, stopping mid-air over Greenland. "What's that down there?"

She narrowed her eyes and gasped. It was one of the beasts, and it appeared to be dead.

Hip opened his eyes and blinked several times, trying to regain consciousness. When he could finally see, he looked around and discovered that he was back inside Aether's cave, on the same couch where he had sat while his arm had healed. The white god of the upper air was sitting on the bed across the table from him, staring.

"What happened?" Hip asked.

"I saved your hide again," the other god said with a smirk.

"How? How did you know where I was?"

"I followed you. I was hoping to catch a glimpse of the other gods when you strolled in, victorious."

Hip rubbed his aching head but managed a smile.

Aether took a sip of wine. "When I saw the Giant attack you, I grabbed him by the tail and dragged him back here."

"You dragged him?"

"He's powerful, but not nearly as fast as we are."

"And you used the herb?"

Aether nodded.

Hip laughed. "Dude. You're amazing."

Aether smiled and shrugged, as if to say, "If the shoe fits, I'll wear it."

Hip felt the duties of Sleep calling to him. "Before I go, I wouldn't mind hearing your story."

Aether scratched his chin. "I'll need you to swear on the River Styx again, that you'll tell no one my name or my whereabouts."

"I swear. But I need to let everyone know I'm okay."

"Just don't mention me."

"I won't."

When Hip reached the Fields of Asphodel, Jen cried tears of relief. She knocked him down in the flowers and held him tight while Muggie lay sleeping beside them. Hip lay there with her on top of him. He stroked her hair and reassured her as she sobbed onto his chest.

At the same time, Hip entered the gates of Mount Olympus and went straight to the main hall, where everyone was gathered, except Poseidon, Demeter, and Dionysus. Hip had never felt so important. Everyone rushed up to embrace him—even Ares, his leg healed. Hip's parents and sisters were there. They all wanted to know what had happened.

"I made the beast vomit," Hip said. "It was disgusting. I don't recommend it."

"Thanks for that advice," Hermes said as he clapped Hip on the back.

"Many of us know the feeling," Hestia said.

Zeus stepped forward. "Do you have any idea who's releasing the Giants, Hypnos?"

"Not yet, but I'm working on it. I've learned how to track the beasts using magnetism and gravity."

"Where did you learn that?" Hades asked him.

"It's hard to explain."

"You're not telling us everything," Apollo said.

Everyone looked at Hip suspiciously.

"Why aren't you being forthright?" Artemis asked.

"What are you holding back?" Hera prodded.

Persephone put her hand on his shoulder. "Hypnos, is everything okay?"

"You're going to have to trust me on this," he said. "I think I'm getting closer to the truth. I'll report back as soon as I know more."

"I don't like the sound of this," Hades said.

Hermes shook his head. "Nor do I."

"Let's give the boy some room." Ares pushed through the crowd. "After all, he came through for me, didn't he?"

Many of the gods nodded.

"I trust you, Hypnos!" Aphrodite cried just before she kissed his cheek.

"Take this," Hephaestus handed over a sheathed sword. "It's made of S7 shock steel—the strongest, sharpest, and most flexible blade I've ever made."

"Thank you," Hip said to the god of the forge.

"And take my shield," Athena said. "But bring it back. Understood?"

"Understood," Hip said. "Thanks." He'd be able to conjure these weapons no matter where he was in the world now that one of him possessed them.

Persephone kissed him on the cheek, and Hades gave him a reassuring nod.

"I'll take my leave, then," he said.

"Report back as soon as possible," Zeus commanded.

Back in the cave, Aether stood up and crossed over to his fireplace, where a fire was already burning a stack of logs. "You'll want some wine. It's a long tale."

"If you insist," Hip said.

Aether grabbed another bottle and poured. "Can you believe I was still using wine skins until about two years ago? I did a favor for Dionysus, and he set me up with cases of this bottled stuff."

Hip took the cup from Aether. "Thanks."

Aether returned to the bed on the other side of the table and sat on the edge, facing Hip, as he'd been before. They each took a drink.

"Very good," Hip said.

"I estimate that I have a few month's supply left," Aether said. "I may need to think up another favor soon."

Hip laughed. "I have a feeling you'll think of something."

Aether shrugged. "So. You want to hear my story?"

Hip nodded. "Especially if it includes your theory about who's letting the Giants out of Tartarus."

"That it does."

Aether leaned his elbows on the wooden table between them and took a deep breath while Hip waited patiently.

"It's not a happy story, Hypnos. Like you, I wanted a son."

"You had a few, didn't you?"

"Yes. Three sons and three daughters. Two of my children—Thalassa and Pontus—took to the sea. Another two—Gaia and Tartarus—became the earth. Of the two left, Aergia—as you know—became the embodiment of laziness, so that left me with my son, Uranus. He joined me in the skies and became the dome of the earth. My son and I spent all our days and nights together until he took Gaia as his wife and began consorting with her."

"I guess marriage tends to do that."

"The problem wasn't that he spent too much time with his wife, Hypnos. The problem was that he became power hungry."

"I'm familiar with his story."

"Yes? Then you know that he buried each of his children as soon as he or she was born."

"Yeah." Hip thought of Muggie and of Hermie and Hestie. He couldn't imagine ever wanting to put them in harm's way for the sake of power. "It's pretty sad."

"Uranus never had a problem putting his needs before anyone else's," Aether continued. "In fact, he seemed to take great pleasure in scheming, tricking, deceiving, and dominating others during the short time he was in power."

"Where were you?" Hip asked. "Why didn't you try to stop him?"

Aether frowned. "I suppose I've always kept to myself. I didn't care about power, and I didn't feel compelled to interfere with my son's plans. Unlike his own son, Cronos, he didn't try to bind me or lock me away with his children. He just ignored me. And over the years, I became indifferent to him and he to me."

Hip shook his head. That same indifference had come over his father and his father's brothers. Zeus, Poseidon, and Hades didn't have the same love and friendship that Hip had for Than and his sisters. And because both Zeus and Poseidon had children from multiple partners—not just one or two but dozens—the family bonds of the other gods didn't seem to be as strong as those between the gods of the Underworld. Hip was grateful for his family and could never imagine ever becoming indifferent to any of them.

"But when Cronos overthrew him, Uranus flew off," Aether continued.

"He rests on Atlas's shoulders now and has for centuries." Hip took another drink of his wine.

"Yes and no."

Hip hated it when people said that. You could say either yes or no, but you couldn't say both. "What do you mean?"

"Atlas holds up the dome of the earth," Aether said. "But just as Gaia can manifest herself as a goddess apart from the earth, Uranus can break from the dome that he embodies."

"Sort of like my power of disintegration?" Hip asked.

"Somewhat—except that unlike you and Death, Earth and Sky can't disintegrate infinitely. They have only the two forms: the embodiment of the earth or of the sky and their godly form. This is true of all the primordial beings, including me."

Hip had never had that explained to him. This must have been what Apollo meant when they'd been discussing Muggie becoming a god. "I know Gaia tends to hang out beneath the city of Delphi—at least that's where Zeus always goes to speak with her."

"Yes. The omphalos. Her belly button. That's where her goddess form tends to live."

"And Uranus?"

"No one knows."

Hip sat back and crossed one leg over the other. "So you think he's the one behind these attacks?"

"I do."

"But why? Why would he release the very beings that he imprisoned centuries ago?"

"That's the million-drachma question."

Hip bit on his lower lip, thinking. What could Uranus gain? Power? "You think he wants to depose Zeus?"

"I can think of no other reason," Aether said.

"But why now?"

"Zeus's reign has been weakened."

"What makes you say that?"

"The other Olympians bound him and forced him to negotiate. Now his power is divided equally between him and his wife, and the domain of the land has been given to his unmarried sisters, Demeter and Hestia."

"Some might say it's made his reign stronger."

"Perhaps," Aether said. "But it's also clear that many are unhappy about what he did to Melinoe. I think Uranus sees an opportunity to turn some of the Olympians to his side."

Hip shook his head. "The others would never want Zeus deposed."

"Even if the new reigning king were your father?"

"Hades?"

Aether nodded.

"Why would Uranus want Hades to rule?"

"Perhaps he believes the only way to succeed is to form an ally with an Olympian. Hades becomes the new king, Zeus is deposed, and Uranus becomes the ruler of the sky again, with a vote on the council at Mount Olympus. This is all speculation, of course."

Hip shifted uncomfortably on the couch. "Has Uranus shared these plans with you?"

"Unfortunately, my son has little to do with me anymore. But I know him well enough to suspect that he's the one releasing the Giants. And I also know that, of the Olympians, he always favored Hades."

"We can speculate all day, but what we need is solid proof."

"We could look for Uranus and question him."

"Do you know where to look?"

"I have a few places in mind, yes."

"I'd like to get the help of the other Olympians."

"Sorry, Hypnos. You either work with them or with me. You're choice."

"You never explained why you don't want the others to know where you are."

Aether took another drink of his wine. "That's an even longer story."

<u>CHAPTER SEVENTEEN</u>

Ambitions

As Jen cried her eyes out on Hip's chest in the Fields of Asphodel, she allowed herself to fall into the deep boon of sleep. She hadn't slept in weeks, so it didn't take long for her to find herself in the Dreamworld.

She stood on top of a cloud in a haze of purple and orange.

Hip moved beside her and whispered, "Really? Of all places, a cloud? I thought we'd be back at your family's ranch in Colorado."

"Figment, I command you to show yourself," she said.

Hip rolled his eyes. "Don't you think *you*, of all people, would get the real thing?"

"Just making sure."

"Come on. I want to show you something."

He took her hand and led her across the cloud from the gates of horn toward the gates of ivory.

Jen stopped. "Why are we going through there?"

"I want you to see Muggie's dream. He's created an amazing fantasy that will never come to be. Come check it out."

Jen followed Hip into a thick beam of bright purple light, which she recognized as the portal through which a god could travel from one person's dream to another. On the other side of the beam, green grass spread out before them, and running through the grass in his new clothes and shoes was Muggie. A figment in the form of Muggie's brother ran beside him, and the two boys were laughing and chasing butterflies.

"Just watch," Hip said. "He'll do it again."

"Do what?"

Hip pointed.

At that moment, Muggie jumped into the air and transformed into a butterfly.

"Did *he* do that, or did you?" Jen asked.

"*He* did it. He controls his own dreams, better than anyone I've ever known before." Then Hip added, "Watch what he does next."

Jen sucked in air as she watched Muggie transform from a butterfly back into himself, but with wings. The butterfly wings flittered from his back and flew him up toward a rainbow in the sky.

"How can he do that?" Jen asked.

"He probably has a divine ancestor somewhere down the line, like Therese."

Jen had forgotten that Therese was a descendant of Eros—which meant she was also a descendant of Aphrodite and Ares, and, of course, Zeus. Maybe that was why it was easier for Therese than it had been for Jen to transition into the life of a goddess.

"This is cute," Hip said. "Watch this. He has a thing for Iris."

Sure enough, a figment in the form of Iris slid down the arch of the rainbow and right into Muggie's outstretched arms. The two were about the same size, and Iris's face had been made younger-looking, like a toddler's. Then the two flew down and each took one of the brother's hands, lifting him into the air. The brother sprouted his own set of wings. Together, they flew from one end of the rainbow to the other with the butterflies trailing behind them.

"Such a beautiful scene," Jen said in awe.

"Now watch me test him." Hip took Jen's hand and led her across the rainbow, after the three flying figures and their flapping wings.

Hip leaned back on Aether's couch with the cup of wine in his hand and waited for the god of the upper air to speak.

"It's a heartbreaking tale, Hypnos. I dread to tell it."

Hip made no reply but took a drink of his wine.

Aether put down his empty cup and refilled it from the bottle. "After my son, Uranus, deserted me, I was alone for many years, until Uranus's daughter Tethys bore the many Nephelae."

"The cloud nymphs."

"Yes." Aether swirled the newly poured wine in his cup. "Back then, they used to fly in their billowing white robes from the seas to the skies, refreshing themselves before raining down their gift of water on the lands."

"But now Iris refills the clouds with water."

"Since the punishment of Prometheus, yes."

"Prometheus?"

Aether nodded. "A sister to the Nephelae, Clymene, bore Prometheus, along with his brothers Epimetheus, Menoetius, and Atlas."

"Yes, I've met them all." Hip cringed at his memory of how Menoetius and Atlas had attempted to overthrow the Olympians last year. The feeling of being trapped in Circe's bed, helpless to stop his brother from delivering the helm to Atlas, still haunted him.

"Then you know that Prometheus and Epimetheus sided with the Olympians during the war and, after, were given the duties of making the animals and humanity, yes?"

Hip nodded. "They say Epimetheus gave all the good gifts to the animals."

"Indeed," Aether said. "The humans were left with no fur, no horns, nothing. They remained in our image."

"Which isn't too shabby, you have to admit." Hip sat back and crossed one leg over the other.

"No, but without our powers, they had little means of protecting themselves from the elements. So, Prometheus gave them fire, and all was well until Zeus demanded that people offer the gods a sacrifice." Aether took another swallow of his wine and lifted the bottle in the air. "More?"

Hip shook his head. "What does all this have to do with your story?"

Aether poured himself another cup. "You see, Prometheus loved his people more than he loved Zeus. You can't blame him, really. Zeus had just trapped most of Prometheus's family in Tartarus."

"Prometheus helped him do it."

"He knew it was either that or be trapped himself. He wasn't stupid."

"The same can't be said for his brother, Epimetheus, and he sided with Zeus, too."

"Touché, my friend. Touché. But the difference between them was that Prometheus was genuinely clever and genuinely kind-hearted, and he had a soft spot for humankind. In fact, the only reason his brother sided with Zeus was because Prometheus begged him to. Prometheus begged all of the Titans to throw down their weapons and join Zeus, but only Epimetheus could be persuaded."

"You sound fond of him."

"I loved Prometheus more than I did any of my own sons."

"And now?"

"After Hercules freed him, Prometheus shunned the gods to live on earth among mortals. I used to keep track of him, but I don't anymore."

"I see."

"When Zeus demanded a ritual sacrifice to keep humanity subservient to the gods, Prometheus tricked him. Did you know that?"

"Of course. Every god knows that story. Prometheus put the best meat in the stomach of an ox, and then he wrapped a bunch of bones with glistening fat. He made the good meat look unappetizing and the bones tasty. Then he asked Zeus to decide which sacrifice humans should make to the gods."

"And as you know, Zeus was fooled into choosing the bones."

"And he was pissed. Do you blame him?"

"I wouldn't have demanded the sacrifice of humanity in the first place," Aether said. "The gods already have everything they need."

Hip took a sip of his wine and gave Aether's answer some thought. The god was right. Why did Zeus even make the demand? Insecurity, Hip supposed. Zeus needed a sign that the people feared him.

Aether cleared his throat. "So, to punish Prometheus, Zeus took fire away from humanity."

"But Prometheus stole it back."

"I know. I gave it to him."

Hip lifted his brows. He hadn't known that.

Aether made his hands go ablaze, like that day he had cauterized Hip's flesh, after the Giant had severed Hip's arm.

"I lit a torch and gave it to Prometheus. I encouraged him to save humanity. From up here, I could see their suffering. They were freezing and starving to death."

"Does Zeus know?"

"I'm sure he suspects it."

"So that's why you keep to yourself?"

"Yes and no."

There was that phrase again. Hip absolutely hated it. "Go on."

"Zeus is impulsive. He doesn't often think before he acts. It's a good thing he has the council of the other Olympians to keep him in check, to some extent. So, yes, I stay away partly from fear of incurring his wrath."

"Only partly?"

"I also don't like him. I don't like the way he rules. I don't like how he treats people and the other gods. I don't want to have anything to do with him or his allies."

"I see."

"I only saved your arm because you needed help, and I could give it. I never intended to become fond of you."

Hip didn't know what to say.

"When Zeus chained Prometheus to that rock and ordered the eagle to eat his liver, every day, indefinitely, I felt as though my heart was being eaten, too."

Hip frowned. He knew what that felt like—having his liver eaten by Zeus's eagle. He shuddered at the memory. He'd only had to endure it once. He couldn't imagine having to endure it day after day, for years.

"The Nephelae and I were flying around together when we heard the frantic clang of chains. We flew to the rock where Prometheus was held prisoner, and he spoke to us. He was terrified, and there was nothing I could do to set him free. Even my fire couldn't melt the adamantine cuffs on his wrists and ankles. All we could do was watch in horror when the bird came and doled its punishment."

Hip's mouth went dry, but his stomach was suddenly too nauseated for wine.

"We cried and screamed with him that day, and for many days after. But after months of this agony, we could no longer bear it. The cloud nymphs flew as far away as they could and refused to return to the sea. I found this cave—it's the furthest point I could find from where Prometheus was chained."

So that's why Iris had to take over the refilling of the clouds. Hip had always wondered about that.

"I felt so guilty for abandoning Prometheus that, when Hercules finally set him free, I couldn't face him."

"You never spoke to him again?"

Aether shook his head. "Like I said, I watched over him for many years—hundreds of years—before I gave up on that."

"It's never too late, you know? You could still try to speak to him."

Aether shook his head and took another drink of his wine. "There's one more piece of the story."

"Oh?"

"Prometheus was also known to have visions, like Apollo. He told Zeus that if he consorted with Thetis, his son would overthrow him. So Zeus avoided her. But when Zeus didn't bother to set him free, Prometheus decided to keep his visions to himself."

"I thought he foretold the prophecy about Metis, Athena's mother. Metis would bear a son that would overthrow Zeus."

"He did. But he didn't tell Zeus until Zeus had already consorted with her. Prometheus did *not* foresee what Zeus would do next."

Hip rubbed at his forehead. Should he believe all that Aether was telling him?

"When Zeus swallowed Metis whole, along with the unborn Athena, Prometheus felt responsible. It's another reason he wanders the earth among the mortals."

The two sat in silence for many minutes. Hip stared at the fire beneath the mantle. Back in the Dreamworld, he'd been testing Muggie, to show the boy's powers to Jen. But now he needed to be calm and quiet. He took Jen's hand and led her back to her own dream, and there he brought forth a figment in the form of Muggie, and he gave himself and Jen the happily ever after that he could only hope would come to pass.

CHAPTER EIGHTEEN

Revelations

When Jen woke up from her dream, she sat up in the Fields of Asphodel and kissed the cheeks of the two boys beside her—Muggie on her left and Hip on her right. She left them sleeping among the flowers to wash up in her rooms, eat a quick bite of food, and head out on Stormy to answer the prayers she'd had to ignore until now.

The first place she went was a small town outside of St. Louis, where a twelve-year-old girl was being taken to stay the weekend with an uncle who'd already mistreated her once. The girl had been too embarrassed and afraid to tell her parents. They'd had no other place to send their daughter while they took their second honeymoon. So, the girl sat quietly in the backseat of the car next to the luggage while her father drove and while her mother talked incessantly about their upcoming cruise.

The parents were driving from Minnesota to Houston, TX, where they would drop off the daughter with the uncle and then head to Galveston to meet their ship. Jen had about twelve hours to figure out what to do.

She flew on Stormy in invisibility mode above the car and listened in on the conversation inside, to see if she could overhear where the uncle lived. If she could find him, she could make him sick—or better, yet, she could make him trip and break both of his legs. Then the parents would have to reschedule their cruise, which would give the girl, and Jen, more time. Jen didn't want to wait until the parents arrived at the uncle's house to do something to the uncle, because she didn't want the girl to have to see him at all.

Jen remembered what it was like being in her father's presence, and she shuddered.

As she listened in on their conversation, she also practiced flying. She climbed from Stormy's back and, gripping his saddle horn, used her toes and one free arm to get her balance. Then, every so often, she'd let go of the saddle horn to fly independently. She wobbled but didn't fall. And that was a good start.

After two hours had gone by and Jen still had heard nothing to help her locate the uncle, she had another idea. She'd beg Poseidon to disrupt the sea and get the cruise canceled. She climbed back on Stormy's saddle and said, "Let's go to the Aegean Sea."

Jen had never gone by herself to Poseidon's palace, and she'd only ever been once. It had been last year, after she and Hip were married. Scylla and Charybdis had instigated a fight with Rhode, and Poseidon had become enraged, because Rhode was his beloved daughter. Helios, Rhode's wife, came up with a peaceful resolution, but Poseidon was so angry, that he wouldn't cooperate. Hypnos and that Pasithea, Hip's ex and the goddess of calm, were ordered by Zeus to go to Poseidon's castle to help him calm down and relax long enough to actually listen to Helios's plan. Jen had insisted that she go, too, because she did not trust the evil Sith lord that was Hip's ex.

Poseidon was like a mad bull when they'd first arrived, but he allowed Hip and Pasithea to work their magic. They'd brought the Muses along to play on their instruments, and the Charities came and massaged Poseidon's feet. By the time it was over, Poseidon was agreeable and had even offered Jen a dolphin ride (she had been talking about how envious she'd been of Therese getting to ride).

So Jen knew where to go. She left Stormy on Rhode's island (Stormy didn't like to swim and was especially nervous of being in water after what had happened recently with Scylla and Charybdis and their evil mother). Rhode was there and offered to keep Stormy company while Jen made her visit to Poseidon.

Jen felt safe swimming directly above Poseidon's castle. None of the monsters would dare attack her here, and even the mortal creatures of the sea in this region should know not to mess with a god. So she enjoyed her swim among the colorful fish as she made her way down to the palace doors. She even remembered to breathe.

The merguards at the door recognized her and let her inside. One of them gave her a bag of rocks to carry to keep her from floating up, and he led her to a chamber and told her to wait. She sat on a spongey chair near a cluster of bright-colored coral and watched the fish swim by on the outside of the transparent castle walls. Jen couldn't recall what the walls were made of. It wasn't glass, but something like adamas, which was a kind of diamond, she thought.

Then another merguard entered and beckoned her to follow him into another room. This chamber was drained of water. She handed over her bag of rocks and took a seat to wait.

In a few more minutes, Poseidon entered. His sun-bleached hair fell to his shoulders. His beard of the same color nearly reached his bare chest, which was tan and golden, like the rest of him. His turquoise eyes were narrowed at her suspiciously. He didn't seem pleased to see her.

"What can I do for you?" he asked as he took a seat on the high throne across from her.

"I need your help," she said. She told him the story about the girl. "If you could disturb the sea in the Gulf of Mexico, then the cruise would be canceled, and the girl saved from being victimized again."

"The only way the cruise would be canceled is if the ship were damaged," Poseidon said. "Do you think that is the best way to solve the problem? To damage a ship of that size will have serious consequences."

"Why wouldn't a *storm* make them postpone or cancel the cruise?" she asked.

"It would have to be a deadly storm, and that would have consequences, too. Is the girl's life worth more than those who would certainly be injured or killed by such a violent storm?"

Jen slowly shook her head. "I guess I didn't think this through far enough." She stood up. "I'm sorry I wasted your time."

"Sit back down, Jen Holt. I'm not finished with you yet."

Her ears burned as she sat back on the chair. Great. She didn't have time for this. Hadn't she mentioned that the girl would be dropped off in a few short hours?

Hip followed Aether from the cave. They flew down the side of the mountain and into a second cave, where a shining chariot of white gold and two gray stallions were waiting. After they stepped into the chariot, Aether took the silver, shining reins and commanded the horses to fly.

They sailed through the clouds over the Baffin Islands, across the Arctic Ocean, toward Alaska.

As they flew, Aether asked, "So what will we do if we find Uranus?"

"Take him to Mount Olympus for questioning," Hip said.

"You don't want to question him yourself first, to confirm my theory?"

"Are you having doubts?"

"I'd rather have proof before you haul him in to Zeus."

"So. you want to interrogate him?"

"No. I think we should spy on him."

Hip sighed. He really wanted to get this over with, but he supposed Aether was right. They should have more proof before they threw around accusations, and, if they questioned Uranus, they'd have no way to tell if the god was answering truthfully.

Aether slowed down the chariot and brought it to a halt on the cliff edge of one of the mountains in northeast Siberia, Russia. Four peaks pointed toward the sky like slender fingers. The stallions landed on one of these and Hip followed Aether from the chariot to the cliff edge, where they gazed down into the snowy gorge below.

"I remember the day you were born," Aether said out of the blue, it seemed.

"You must have an excellent memory."

Aether laughed. "Perhaps, but the reason I can vividly recall yours and your brother's births is because of how determined Hera was to bring you harm."

Hip crossed his arms at his chest and lifted his chin. He'd never heard such a thing. "Why would Hera want to do that?"

Aether opened his eyes wide with surprise. "You've never heard the story of your own birth?"

Hip shook his head.

"You never asked your mother or your father to tell it to you?" Aether put his hands on his hips.

"I may have asked when I was younger. I can't remember."

"Hera wanted revenge on your father for helping the Trojans during the long war."

"But my father was neutral."

"I know that, and you know that, but Hera was convinced otherwise."

"What could possibly give her that idea?"

"Achilles wanted to get back at Agamemnon for taking away his war prize, so he asked his mother to convince Zeus to help the Trojans."

"I'm familiar with that story."

"Your father had gone to the front to watch, and he ran into Hera. She was worried about what would befall the Greeks if Zeus went against them, so Hades gave her the idea to distract Zeus at home. 'Make love to your husband,' he said."

"That was good advice."

"Yes, it was. But then Artemis accused your father of playing favorites. She reminded him that she had searched hours and hours for your sisters, who flew off as soon as they were born, and Hera had done nothing to help."

Hip hadn't known that about his sisters, and noticing Hip's surprise, Aether added, "Oh, you didn't know that, either? Yes, your sisters were known as the Kindly Ones, because as soon as they were born, they flew to the battlefields to bring blessings to the sick and dying."

"I think you may have had too much wine, old man," Hip teased.

"Just hear me out, Hypnos. I am shocked that you've never been told this."

"I'll hear you out, but I can't promise I'll believe you."

"Fair enough." Aether cupped a hand to his chin. "Let me see. Artemis wanted a speedy end to the war. So Hades agreed to help convince Athena and the others supporting the Greeks to let Paris and Menelaus fight it out alone. The victor would determine the winner of the Trojan War. Everyone was tired of fighting, you see."

"I know the story," Hip said. "Menelaus would have won had Aphrodite not flown away with Paris."

"Paris had chosen Aphrodite as the most beautiful of the goddesses, so he'd become her special pet."

"So why would Hera blame my father?"

"Because if she hadn't taken his advice, she would have been there to stop Aphrodite."

"That doesn't seem fair at all."

"As your father always says…" Aether gave Hip a smile. Hip nodded and smiled back, surprised that Aether knew his father's saying, *Life isn't fair, but Death is.*

Aether continued, "And so the day your mother went into labor, Hera tried to bring harm to you and your brother. Your mother fled with Hecate to the island of Delos. Dione helped, too. She created a wall of water to hide you, but Hera broke through it, and it nearly washed you away."

"If what you say is true, it might explain why I hate the water so much."

"Indeed. Your brother saved your life. Then Hera sent the Harpies down, and they snatched you and your brother from your mother's clutches and carried you off."

"Seriously? Why can't I remember any of this?"

"I don't know the answer to that, Hip. But I witnessed Artemis save you from the Harpies when she shot them each with her arrows. And I saw you carried back to Mount Olympus. And later, I heard that you'd been named Gelos, because you brought merriment to all in your company, and your brother, who was born first and who helped to save your life, was called Zao, for life."

Hip shook his head. None of it made a bit of sense. "But why? Why would our names change later?"

"When Melinoe was born with her deformities, she accused your father of trying to kill her while she was still in your mother's womb. Apollo, Tiresias, and other prophets had had visions of Hades bringing harm to his unborn child."

"Zeus confessed…"

"Only recently. But centuries ago, he let your father take the blame. Not only did Hades take the blame for Zeus's crime, but your entire family was punished for it. Instead of blessings, your sisters were to bring vengeance. Instead of laughter and merriment, you were to put people to sleep. Instead of life, your brother was to bring death."

Hip shook his head again and again, backing away from Aether in disbelief. "That can't be right. Even Zeus couldn't be that heartless."

"If you don't believe me, ask your father," Aether said. "Now let's stop talking as we move down the mountain, so we don't alert Uranus, just in case he's where I think he is."

Back in the Underworld, Hip disintegrated and sought his parents in their palace.

"Who told you this?" Persephone asked.

"Just tell me if it's true," Hip demanded.

"It's true." Hades sat down on his throne and tugged at his beard.

Hip stood before him, bewildered. "But why would you hide this from me? Why don't I remember?"

"We allowed your memories to be erased." Persephone took her seat beside Hades. "We thought you'd be sad all your days if you compared the happiness of your early life to what followed."

"I want my memories back," Hip demanded. "You had no right to take them from me in the first place."

"It was Athena's idea," Hades said.

"Apollo said you'd be healthier *without* your memories," Persephone added.

"We did what we thought was best at the time," Hades said. "But I suppose we can ask the council if, in light of Zeus's confession, your memories can be restored."

"Thank you," Hip said. "I would like that."

Hades nodded. "The question is whether we should give your brother and sisters the same choice."

"Maybe we should wait and see how Hypnos feels once *his* memories are returned," Persephone said sadly.

Hip frowned. Surely the memories wouldn't make him so devastated that he'd ever agree with his parents. He hoped he was making the right decision. Now that he knew they'd been taken way, his curiosity was overwhelming.

The only thing Jen could imagine Poseidon would want to discuss was what had gone down between her and Scylla. "If this is about Scylla…"

"Indeed."

"I was trying to do my job. She's a victim, you know."

"Why are you so defensive, like a child? You think I mean to scold you?"

Jen didn't know what to say.

"Very little goes on in my waters without my knowledge, Jen Holt. I admire your courage and your dedication to your duties."

She hid her surprise. "I could have used your help when Keto tried to feed me to her husband."

"Who do you think forced Charybdis to vomit you onto that island?"

Jen's mouth dropped open.

"That's right," Poseidon said. "Keto meant to take you all the way to her castle. Why would she make Phorcys come out to an island? It was because I intervened."

"I was still nearly swallowed."

"But you weren't."

"Someone else saved me." As soon as she'd spoken, she realized she'd said too much. Hip had told her she wasn't to speak of it.

"Who?"

"I don't know."

"That's what I want you to find out," he said. "If you want my help in saving that girl, I want you to use your relationship with Scylla to get information for me."

"But you said you couldn't help me."

"Not by damaging a ship or creating a storm, but I never said I wouldn't help."

"What kind of information?"

"I think the Old Man of the Sea and his wife know who's been attacking Gaia."

"I think so, too." Jen recalled what Keto had told her. "They didn't know anything when they were questioned by Apollo, but later, I think they found out something."

"Whoever is doing this wants to take over Mount Olympus," Poseidon said. "There's no other reason. This is serious, Jen Holt. We need to use everything in our arsenal to protect our way of life."

"But what can I do? Scylla hates me now."

"I want you to reach out to her again and offer her another chance. Get her to trust you again. Then maybe she'll turn on her mother and tell us what we need to know."

Jen took a deep breath and let it out. "I'll do it, but it's going to take me a long time. I may not even succeed. This girl only has a couple of hours before she's put in harm's way."

"I'll take you on your word, Jen Holt," Poseidon said. "Those sons of Ares owe me a favor. I'll send them to the girl."

"What sons?"

"Phobos and Deimos. Do you not know them?"

"Fear and Panic? They tried to kill my best friend. Why would we send them to a helpless twelve-year-old?" Jen wondered if she should trust the god of the sea after all.

"Fear and Panic aren't all bad," he said. "In fact, they often save lives."

Jen looked back at him skeptically.

"Fear makes a person flee from danger," Poseidon explained. "Panic makes a mother rush her child to medical care. That surge of adrenaline that can make a father lift a car to save his child—that comes from Phobos and Deimos."

"Oh," Jen said. "So how will they help the girl?"

"You'll see soon enough," he said. "And to show you I'm not just a bull-headed god full of hot steam, I'll even go with you to watch the boys in action."

Jen still wasn't sure this would work, but she had no better plan.

CHAPTER NINETEEN

Seek and Find

Hip searched for Muggie in the Dreamworld and followed him around, admiring his ability to transform seamlessly from one thing to another. Muggie was a butterfly one moment and then a dragon, a bird one minute and a turtle the next; but always he was flying. And more often than not, he transformed his figments into Iris.

But just now, Hip was moved to tears as Muggie landed in a field of flowers, similar to the Fields of Asphodel, and took the hands of two figments that resembled Hip and Jen. The three strolled through the flowers, hand in hand, until they came to a fourth figure. It was the boy's brother. The figment who resembled Hip took the brother in his arms. Then Jen picked up Muggie, and the four of them entered a cozy house together.

To Hip, this meant that Muggie wanted the same thing he and Jen wanted. This filled him with even greater determination. Although he couldn't bring the boy's brother back from the dead, he would do whatever he could to make part of Muggie's dream come true.

Jen clung with white knuckles to the edge of Poseidon's chariot as the three white mares—Seaquake, Riptide, and Crest—lifted the chariot from the ocean and into the crisp blue sky. They shot through the clouds directly for Mount Olympus, where they circled the summit until they saw Ares's chariot behind them. Holding the reins was one of the twins—Jen couldn't tell which. They stood side by side with their thick, red hair dancing like fire around their faces, their intense black eyes smoldering like coal. They could be blazing suns, Jen thought—or better yet, lions, their hair like manes.

"This way!" Poseidon shouted as he directed the chariot toward North America.

Then Poseidon turned to Jen. "Do you know where we're going?"

"Texas," she said.

"Could you be more specific? That's a big state."

"Let's start in Waco and then follow the highway toward Houston."

In a flash, they were flying above Waco. Jen looked back to see the twins still behind them. She gazed down over the edge of the chariot at the cars along the highway. Then she heard a prayer from the very girl she was looking for. She sounded close to Houston.

"Faster," Jen said. "I think they're on the edge of the city."

Like lightening ripping across the sky, they shot through the air toward Houston. Jen spotted the car and pointed. The twins abandoned their chariot and entered the car—one in the backseat beside the girl, and the other in the front between the two parents. They were invisible to the mortals, but their presence had an immediate impact on everyone in the car. Jen watched on with a mixture of hope and worry.

"What if I feel claustrophobic in our tiny cabin?" the father asked from behind the wheel.

"I hadn't thought of that," the mother said. "But *I've* been secretly worried about everyone on board getting sick. I've heard so many awful stories, and suddenly I feel terrified that might happen to *us*."

Jen watched the girl in the backseat begin to squirm and shift uncomfortably. Her hands were trembling, and tears had begun to fall down her cheeks.

"Then don't go," the girl said. "Please."

The mother turned to look at her daughter. "Paula? What's wrong?"

Paula broke down into sobs.

"Honey, maybe you should pull over," the mother said to the father.

"That's not a bad idea."

Jen watched from Poseidon's chariot as the car took the next exit and pulled into a gas station.

By this time the girl was sobbing uncontrollably. The mother got out of the car and opened the door behind her. Then she climbed into the backseat beside her daughter, unknowingly squishing one of Ares's sons between them.

"Paula, please talk to me," the mother said.

"It's Uncle George," Paula said as she covered her face. "He's not nice to me."

The father leaned closer to his daughter from behind the wheel. "What do you mean? He yells at you? He hits you? What?"

Paula shook her head. "Worse."

Jen didn't want to stay to hear the details. "Let's go."

Poseidon pulled the reins and shouted, "To Rhode!"

"Are you ready to give this a try?" Therese asked her aunt and uncle from their deck, beneath the two giant Elm trees.

Her parents were perched on the lowest branches, twittering away. She longed for the days when she could understand what they were saying.

Hermie and Hestie stood beside her, looking up and listening intently.

"Slow down," Hermie said to the birds. "We can't understand you when you speak that quickly."

"This has got to be a joke," Richard said. "And a cruel one."

"Calm down, dear," Carol said.

Than clapped his hand on Richard's shoulder. "I know it's hard to believe, but we're telling you the truth."

Lynn had remained inside. It was her naptime. Carol and Richard weren't ready to share any of this new information with her yet.

The two redbirds sang a slower song.

"That's incredible!" Carol said. "They slowed down their tune!"

Hestie tugged on Carol's hand. "She's asking me to remind you about the time Blue ate your birthday cake."

Carol looked at Therese. "Did you tell Hestie that story?"

Therese shook her head. "It's one I don't think I've heard."

Carol backed up, waving her hands. "I love you, sweetheart, but I need more proof that this isn't some twisted joke, or that you aren't all going insane or something. Tell the bird to tell us something no one else would know."

Hermie said to the birds, "But who's that? What?"

Hestie asked, "Brian Pierce?"

Carol's face went pale. "Okay. No need to say more."

"Who's Brian Pierce?" Richard asked.

"We'll talk about that later." Carol looked as though she might faint. Her eyes filled with tears. "It must be true. Everything you're saying must be true!"

Therese hugged her aunt. The birds fluttered in the air above their heads. Therese held out her finger, and her father landed on it.

With a trembling hand, Carol did the same. Than cupped his hand around hers and steadied it.

The other bird perched on Carol's finger.

"That's my mom," Therese said. "And this is my dad."

The bird Therese was holding softly bit her ear, tickling her. She giggled. And when she looked over at Carol, she saw her aunt was studying the bird with open curiosity, willing herself to believe.

Poseidon flew his chariot back to Rhode's island, where Stormy and Rhode were waiting. Poseidon invited his daughter to come to the palace for a visit, and she accepted. They waved goodbye as Seaquake, Riptide, and Crest cut like a knife through the sky and into the sea.

As Jen mounted her horse, feeling satisfied that she'd saved another child, Hades appeared in his chariot.

"What business did you have with Poseidon?" he asked.

Jen told him about the deal she'd made—how Phobos and Deimos had helped save the girl, Paula, and how Jen was now going to see if she could reconnect with Scylla.

"I don't like that idea one bit," Hades said. "Why do Zeus and Poseidon want to put *my* children at risk and none of their own?"

Was Hades referring to *her* as one of his children? Did he actually think of her as a daughter? She studied him and realized that was precisely what he had meant. This amazing, powerful god loved her. She didn't think her heart could be any more joyful. It had been years since she felt anything close to a father's love. Mr. Stern was a wonderful man, but by the time he'd come into Jen's mother's life, Jen had moved away.

Tears stung her eyes. She quickly wiped them away and cleared her throat. "I hadn't thought of it that way."

"It's a good idea, though. I must admit," Hades said. "But I don't want you to go alone, understand?"

"Won't Scylla become suspicious if I bring someone else along with me?"

Hades glanced around the island. Then he put a finger to his lips before sliding on his helm. He and his chariot disappeared.

He slipped off the helm and winked at her. "Are we in accord?"

Jen couldn't hold back her grin. "Should I head for Scylla's cave now?"

"Not yet. Climb aboard. Stormy can go home. I'm looking for Hip, and you may as well join me."

"Looking for Hip? All we have to do is call him."

"Don't," Hades said. "I don't want him to know I'm looking for him."

"Why?" Jen climbed from Stormy's back and joined Hades in the chariot.

"I'll explain on the way," he said.

Hip followed Aether down into a deep icy gorge between the four mountain peaks resembling fingers. Once they neared the bottom, Aether stopped and listened. Then he signaled to Hip to stay put. Aether flew to the entrance of the cave and, after a moment, beckoned Hip to follow.

The cave was larger than Aether's but similar in layout, with a rock hearth for a fire in the back and a square table between two daybeds. Uranus was not in the cave, but there were signs that he'd been there recently. There was a corked bottle of wine on the table and a golden goblet. Two bowls sat next to them—one full of empty peanut shells and another with two black olives.

"We could wait nearby to see if he returns." Aether popped one of the olives into his mouth. He offered Hip the other, and, when Hip declined, Aether ate that one, too.

Hip supposed it wouldn't hurt to hang out somewhere near the cave to keep watch.

"Why don't you have a seat for a minute while I look for clues?" Aether suggested. "Maybe he keeps a journal or has a map or something that might reveal his plans."

"I should help you search," Hip said.

"If you wish, though this is where he would keep his papers. In this chest."

"What's that?" Hip pointed near the hearth to a golden chair that resembled a throne. "Was that once Uranus's throne?"

"I'm glad you asked. It's much more than a throne. Try it out."

As soon as Hip had sat on it, chains twined around his ankles and chest like white snakes, and he reintegrated into the one prisoner. He realized at that moment that he had sat on the trick throne Hephaestus had once made for Hera, to get his revenge on her for throwing him from Mount Olympus when he was born. Why was it here, in the sky god's cave? And wasn't Hephaestus the only soul who could release the throne's prisoner?

"What are you up to?" Hip asked the other god.

Aether grinned. "I have something important to tell you, my friend."

CHAPTER TWENTY

Enlightenment

Although it seemed to Jen that Poseidon drove his chariot much faster than Hades drove his, Hades liked to turn on a dime, making for a jolty ride. Jen held on for dear life as Hades wove in and out through the cold mountains of northern Alaska.

"I need to fly close to the valleys if I'm to sense his presence," Hades explained. "Are you okay?"

Jen nodded but gripped the side of the chariot so hard it hurt. "Wouldn't it be easier just to ask Hip where he is?"

"I'm sure he can't tell us," Hades replied. "When he last spoke to me, I could tell he was holding something back."

"Me, too."

"What exactly did he tell you?"

Jen hesitated.

"Did you swear an oath?" Hades asked.

She shook her head. "He just asked me not to repeat what he said."

"But it may save his life, Jen. Please tell me everything you know."

She bit her lip. What choice did she have? If she kept her word to Hip, it could cost him his life—at least, that's what Hades believed. The worst that could happen if she did spill the beans was that Hip would be angry with her. But she'd rather risk that than his life.

"He said someone helped him find Ares's leg. He taught him about how to use changes in magnetism and gravity."

"Who?"

"Hip wouldn't say, but he said the god had helped the Olympians overthrow Cronos, and that he likes to keep to himself. He only helped Hip because one of the Giants almost ate Hip's arm."

"Hypnos almost lost an arm?"

Jen nodded. "And the god gave the Giant an herb that made it vomit up Ares's leg. Then he distracted the monster while Hip got the leg and brought it to Mount Olympus."

"Why would this god wish to maintain anonymity if he's helping?"

Jen shrugged. "All Hip said was that the god likes to stay under the radar." Then she added, "And that he knows things."

"Something's wrong with this picture," Hades said. "At first, I suspected someone like Uranus, but he definitely did not help us overthrow my father."

"Is there anyone else you can think of?"

"There are many possibilities, but the sky gods are the best suspects, given where the Giants were spotted and the way they escaped. I've kept a strict watch over my domain, so the god must come from water or sky. I wonder if Helios could tell me anything."

"Can we go ask him?"

"We're headed in his direction now." Hades guided his horses around another mountain peak. "I've always worried about my sons because of their powers of disintegration. If someone wanted to overthrow Zeus, Hypnos and Pete would be powerful weapons."

Jen thought she was going to be sick, and not because of the jolty ride. "You think this god is using Hip? Do you think he's going after Pete, too?"

"I hope not, but I intend to find out."

Just then, Jen felt the duties of Sleep take possession of her, and a cold finger of terror traced down her back. "Oh, no!"

Hades looked at her and immediately recognized what had happened. "My son's in grave danger, Jen. You have to help me find him."

"I really have grown fond of you, Hypnos," Aether said. "I'm sorry to abuse you this way, but I can think of no alternative."

Hip squirmed against the chains to no avail. "No alternative to what?"

"I need to possess your body, so I can use your powers to take over Mount Olympus."

Hip reached out in prayer to his father and mother—to all of the gods on Mount Olympus—but no one replied. Was he blocked? He kicked against the chains around his ankles. "So, everything you told me was a lie."

"Not everything. I was honest about my hatred for Zeus and his allies."

"I don't recall you using the word 'hatred.'"

"*Dislike*, rather."

"Very different things."

"And I was also honest about my desire to make your father the new king of the Olympians."

"You said that was your *son's* desire. You never said you wanted the same thing."

The god clicked his tongue and shook his head, like a schoolmaster chiding a pupil. "And, if your father is willing to work with me, that could still one day be. You see, I have great respect for Hades. It's the other Olympians whom I despise."

"Then set me free, and I'll go with you to speak to him."

Aether smiled. "No, I think I'll keep you here as a bargaining chip."

"Do you really expect Hades to become an ally of someone who's kidnapped his son?" Hip asked.

"The Olympians were quick to forgive Zeus for what he did to your family, were they not? He was even forgiven by Athena for having swallowed her for her entire childhood, and then he kidnapped her to avoid having to free Metis. Did Athena hold that against her dear old dad? Apparently not."

Hip realized Aether was right. It was also true that Hip had helped to bind Zeus to make him cooperate with the Athena Alliance. Isn't that what Aether was doing to him? "You make sound arguments. I'm sure my father will hear you out."

"I'm certain of it, too. He'll have to, if he wants to get his son back." Aether took a needle and syringe and injected it into Hip's arm.

Hip squirmed and gritted his teeth, but there was nothing he could do to stop the needle from penetrating his flesh. "What's that?"

"Dark magic." The god turned his hand into flames and sterilized the needle before injecting himself. "We'll take this potion every four hours for one full day."

"And then what?"

"Our souls will become malleable but not to the extent that they'll call to Death," Aether explained. "Then it will be easy for me to switch bodies with you. Once I control your body, I can disintegrate and take prisoners, one by one, by surprise, leaving your father to the last. By then, he'll have no choice but to come over to my side."

"How do you know this potion will work?" Hip asked.

"I've used it before, my friend," Aether said. "You see, this isn't my body."

Jen sat beside Hades in his chariot as they flew up to meet Helios in the bright sky, and, simultaneously, Jen searched for any gods who might be sleeping in the Dreamworld, to alert them.

"Hypnos is missing," she whispered to Artemis and Apollo. "Please wake up and help me find him."

She also ran throughout the Underworld and got Persephone, Hecate, Pete, Tizzie, Alecto, and Meg to help with the search. Together, she and Pete disintegrated and combed the earth. Her brother knew she couldn't fly, so he held her where they searched by sky. She told him what Hades had said about Pete being in danger, that she didn't want him going anywhere alone until this crisis was over.

At the same time as she was rallying the help of the Underworld gods and flying with Pete, Jen disintegrated and god traveled to Mount Olympus. Once she was through the gates, she rushed into the main hall and shouted her message without hiding from the Fear and Panic that had gripped her heart, because she now understood that even they could be her friends.

While she was in the palace on Mount Olympus, where all the other gods and goddesses were leaving to search for Hip, except for the seasons, who would guard the gates, she prayed to Phobos and Deimos to come and help her.

The twins appeared, full of smiles.

"I still don't know how to fly," she told them, trembling even more in their presence than she had been before their arrival. "But right now, I'm more afraid of losing Hip than I am of losing control in the air."

"What do you want us to do?" Deimos asked.

"Fly with me," she said through chattering teeth. "So I can harness that fear and use it to my advantage."

Together, the three of them walked through the gates of Mount Olympus to the edge of the summit.

"Ready?" Phobos asked.

In the Fields of Asphodel, she clung to Muggie and kissed his curls as her entire body was wracked with sobs; but, on the summit of Mount Olympus, she nodded fiercely to Fear and Panic and said, "Let's do this!"

"So, which is it?" Hip asked his kidnapper after he'd been injected for the second time. "Are you Aether? Or is that Aether's body?"

"I needed these." The god turned his hands ablaze. "So I could open up the volcanoes and release the Giants. They're also good for cooking," he shot a flame at the stacks of logs in the hearth, "and for sterilizing needles." He laughed as he injected himself.

"And whose body did you take?"

The god returned his hands to normal. "Aether's."

"Then who are *you*?"

"Dear Hypnos, if you can't guess by now, you don't deserve to know."

"You only saved my arm because you needed it."

"You have plenty of time to work it all out, my friend," the god said. "Neither of us will be leaving this cave for another twenty hours, and then only one of us, and it won't be you."

"Quit calling me your friend. You are the opposite of my friend."

"Not true, Hypnos. Not true at all. You see, I believe we will be allies one day."

"That will never happen."

"We'll see what your father has to say about that." The god cupped a hand on Hip's shoulder and leaned close. "And there's something else you should know."

Aether stepped back and held out his hand to a figure who was just now entering the mouth of the cave. Hypnos squinted against the early dawn light, his godly vision impaired by the trick throne and whatever dark magic was being used on him.

As the figure moved closer, Hip saw it was Athena's mother. That seemed impossible to Hip. Surely she would only be here against her will. "Metis? Is that you? Or has someone else inhabited your body?"

"It's me, Hypnos," the goddess said. "Though someone else *does* inhabit my body." She rubbed her belly affectionately.

"Guess what, my friend?" the other god said. "Metis is pregnant with Zeus's son, the one who Prometheus said would overthrow the Olympian king."

Hip's mouth fell open, and his stomach became a ball of knots. "That's not possible. Hera made everyone sterile."

"We used Circe's dark magic," the god said. "I had to use the bones of two hundred mortals, but I think it was worth it in the end."

"But Zeus would never…" His voice dropped off, because he no longer knew what Zeus was capable of.

"I disguised myself as Hera," Metis explained.

"Why?" Hip asked. "How could you betray us like this?"

"I'm not betraying *you*, Hypnos," she said sweetly. "I'm saving you from a tyrannical ruler."

Hip jutted his chin. "I thought you loved Zeus."

"I suppose you could say I've been enlightened," Metis said with an affectionate glance toward the other god, whoever he was.

The other god grinned.

As Jen sat beside Hades while he questioned the sun god, she also soared over Greece—half flying and half falling. Phobos and Deimos flew on either side of her, reminding her that Hip's life depended on her.

Deimos grabbed her arm to help her avoid grazing a mountain peak. "Hypnos could be trapped forever, Jen. Get serious about this."

"He needs you now more than ever," Phobos shouted.

Her heartbeat quickened, and all the moisture left her mouth. Her throat nearly closed, and she could barely breathe. At the same time, she became frantic and bold and wildly determined. She pushed herself higher in the sky and commanded the air around her like never before. In that moment, she realized that fear and bravery were two sides of the same thing.

"That's it!" Phobos shouted. "You're doing it!"

"Now go and rescue your husband!" Deimos said.

She let go of Pete as they flew all over the earth—on the light side as well as the dark. Pete cried out a congratulatory "Look at you!" As much as she wanted to rejoice in her newfound victory over her fear of flight, she was way too frightened for Hip, and she was equally determined to find him.

At the same time as she'd been learning to fly, Jen had gone with Hades to see Helios, who couldn't recall the last time he had seen Hypnos. He had recommended that they go and ask Selene. So, Jen gripped the side of the chariot as Hades weaved in and out of all the mountains of North America and Europe, and then headed south across Africa, where Selene appeared in the distance.

When they questioned the moon goddess about Hip, she said, "I saw him hours and hours ago over Northern Siberia."

Hades pulled on the reins and sped like a bullet to Russia while every fragmented Jen flocked to that region like a massive army. Pete went with her. At the same time, she alerted the other Olympians, and every one of them—except Zeus—replied that they were on their way.

Lord Zeus? she prayed, feeling utterly disappointed. *Aren't you with us?*

She didn't hear from him for many minutes, but, just when she feared she wouldn't get his help, he replied, *I've found something.*

CHAPTER TWENTY-ONE

Aether

Jen continued to search the Siberian mountains for Hip with Pete and the other gods while she also went to Mount Olympus, where Zeus and Poseidon were waiting with their prisoner.

The god was bound at the wrists and ankles and was encased by Poseidon's golden net.

As soon as Hades charged inside, full of anger and vengeance, he narrowed his eyes at his brothers' prisoner. "Uranus!"

"Like I told Zeus, I'm not Uranus," the god insisted.

Apollo and Aphrodite entered as the prisoner spoke, followed by Hera.

"He speaks the truth," Apollo said.

"Then who is this?" Hera demanded.

"He says he's Aether," Zeus replied. "We found him bound at the wrists and ankles in one of Uranus's caves."

"But how can he be Aether?" Aphrodite asked. "Poseidon's net would reveal any god who's disguised as another."

"Dark magic," the prisoner said.

"Where's Hecate?" Aphrodite asked Hades. "She might know what to do."

"She's with Persephone, searching the mountains of Siberia. I don't think I can reach her telepathically from this distance."

Hera summoned Iris from the rainbow over Mount Olympus and told her to find Hecate.

"Do you know where Uranus is keeping Hypnos prisoner?" Hades asked the god in the net.

"No."

"He speaks the truth," Apollo said.

Jen's heart sank in her chest. She couldn't stop trembling.

"Do you know why your son did this to you?" Zeus asked Aether.

"He means to overthrow you," the prisoner answered.

Again, Apollo said, "He speaks the truth."

"How?" Hera asked.

"He wanted my body so he could use my hands of fire to release the Giants," Aether explained. "My hands were meant to keep the stars twinkling. They were *not* meant to start a war."

"Why weren't the Giants sent to attack Mount Olympus?" Poseidon asked.

"I think the answer to that question is obvious," Hades said. "He wanted to lure my sons."

Aether nodded. "You're right, Lord Hades. Uranus knew that the Olympians would go after the beasts. He also knew that if a god or part of a god were swallowed by one of them, the gods of disintegration would be told to search."

"Again, he speaks the truth," Apollo said.

Jen covered her mouth, trying hard not to be sick. She looked at one god after another and said, "Please don't let him hurt Hypnos. Please help him."

"Uranus doesn't intend to hurt him," Aether said to Jen in a surprisingly kind voice.

Jen wiped her tears from her cheeks and asked, "How do you know? Are you sure?"

"He intends to take over Hypnos's body, so he can use his power of disintegration and pose as him," Aether replied.

"Exactly how is he planning to use Hypnos's power?" Zeus asked.

"Uranus plans to deceive all of you into trusting him, so he can take you, one by one, by surprise."

"That's a clever plan," Apollo said. "But now that we know the truth, he won't succeed."

"He won't be able to trick you, no," Aether said. "But he may still be victorious."

"How?" Hera asked.

"By amassing an army using Hip's power," Jen said.

"No, that's not it," Aether said.

"Then spit it out, old man," Poseidon raged just as Iris arrived with Hecate.

"We all know that as soon as *one* is trapped or badly injured, the rest of the army re-integrates, so that can't be it," Aether pointed out.

"Go on," Zeus prodded.

"Uranus plans to turn the other Olympians against you, Zeus." Aether said.

Jen glanced around the room at the shock on everyone's faces.

Hera took her husband's hand. "That will never happen."

"He intends to make promises to Hades and to Poseidon," Aether continued.

"I won't betray my king," Poseidon said.

Zeus turned to Hades for his support.

Hades stared back at Zeus for an awkward moment and then said, "That's a foolish ambition."

To Jen, Zeus did not seem reassured.

"You may be right," Aether said. "My son knew you might find me and interrogate me, so, although he mentioned an ace in the hole, he did not reveal to me what it is."

"He speaks the truth," Apollo said.

"An ace in the hole?" Aphrodite gasped. "What could it be?"

The gods looked from one to another, but none had any ideas.

Hip clenched his fists. "You know the other gods are searching for me, don't you?"

The white god injected him with more of the potion. "Maybe they are. Maybe they aren't. They didn't find you the last time you lost your power of disintegration." The god used his flaming hand to sterilize the needle before injecting himself. "Stings a little, doesn't it?"

"Where did you get that potion, anyway?" Hip asked.

"Where does anyone get good dark magic?" The god sat on the bed beside Metis.

"From Circe's house," Metis replied. "He's seen her use it before, haven't you, my dear?"

"Many times," the god answered. "As soon as the Olympians imprisoned her in Tartarus, I took what potions I wanted. That's also where I found the herb that made the Giants vomit."

"You're very resourceful," Metis said to the god.

The god smiled and squeezed her hand.

"Maybe I can believe you'd turn on Zeus," Hip said to Metis. "But I can't believe you'd turn on your own daughter."

"How dare you!" Metis said, her eyes wide. "My daughter will know whose side to take. Like me, she was gifted with wisdom. And if you were wise, Hypnos, you'd join us, too."

"Is there anything else you can tell us?" Hades asked the prisoner still enveloped in Poseidon's net on Mount Olympus.

Jen held her breath, begging the god telepathically to help anyway he could.

"When did Hypnos lose his power of disintegration?" Aether asked Jen.

"Um," she glanced at Hades, having no idea how much time had gone by.

"About eight hours ago," Hades said.

"Then you have sixteen hours to find him before my son's soul takes possession of your son's body," Aether said to Hades. "And even now, it may be too late to stop the process. I don't know."

"That sounds like one of Circe's potions," Hecate said. "I know she also had an antidote among the bottles at her lair."

Jen flew to Hecate and took her by the shoulders. "I stole a bunch of Circe's bottles for Scylla and have them in my room. Would you recognize the antidote if you saw it?"

"No, but I would if I smelled it," Hecate said. "It has a distinct odor."

"Then let's go!"

Jen and Hecate flew to Jen's rooms, where Jen grabbed her bag from a hook by the door. She laid the bottles out on the couch. Hecate uncorked and sniffed each one—there was at least a dozen different colored liquids. Jen watched on, holding her breath.

"None of these is the antidote," Hecate said. "I'll have to go to Circe's house and search through her things. Are you coming?"

Jen hesitated. If one of Circe's booby traps took away her power of disintegration, Jen wouldn't be able to continue to help in the search for Hip. But she supposed, in that case, her power would be given to another, and maybe that god would be more capable.

She studied Hecate for a moment and realized the other goddess hadn't hesitated to ask for her help. Hecate believed in her. It was time Jen believed in herself.

"Yes," she finally said.

CHAPTER TWENTY-TWO

Return to Circe's Lair

Therese stretched in bed beside Than after waking from a troubling dream. She'd tried several times to command the figment to show itself, but it hadn't worked. Lately, her dreams hadn't been as lucid as they were in the past. She found herself having less and less control.

Than opened his eyes and caught her staring at him. They both smiled.

"Good morning," he said.

"Good morning," she reached over and kissed him.

"I'm surprised you're up this early."

On Sundays, they usually slept until the twins woke them up by running in all at once and fighting for the middle spot between mommy and daddy.

"I had a bad dream," she admitted.

"Oh, yeah? Me, too. What was yours about?"

She nestled her head in the crook of his arm and ran her fingers through his chest hair. "It was so vivid. I was marching in my high school band, playing my flute, like I used to."

"You haven't played in a long time."

"I know, right? Anyway, I kept forgetting my steps. I was getting more and more confused and bumping into other band members. And then my flute turned into Muggie's toothbrush, but I was still trying to play it."

"I bet that wasn't easy." Than laughed.

"That's not the bad part. Jen appeared in the middle of the football field during our number, but she wasn't in her band uniform or playing her French horn."

"Jen was in my dream last night, too," Than said.

"Really? Well, in my dream, she told me that Hip had been captured by Uranus and all the gods were trying to find him before Uranus took over Hip's body."

Than stiffened beside her.

"Than?" Therese sat up and studied her husband. He'd turned nearly as white as their sheets. "Than, are you okay?"

"That's the same thing Jen said to me in my dream."

Jen hovered in the bright sky directly above Circe's island.

"I can feel the dark magic all over her house," Hecate said beside her.

"Now that I can fly, I won't fall into the same trap," Jen said. "Let's go."

"Wait," Hecate warned. "There's definitely more than one kind of trap. We need a protection spell."

"Okay. How long will that take?"

"I can get everything I need here, except a glass jar and the blood of a dragon."

"Huh? We don't have time for that."

"Better safe than sorry," Hecate said. "Go grab a glass jar with a lid from anywhere and then go to Ladon. Put him and the Hesperides into the deep boon of sleep before you prick him with your sword and collect his blood in the jar. I just need a drop."

"This is insane," Jen objected. Did Hecate really think Jen could do all that? She'd only just learned to fly. "Let's just get in and out, real quick."

"Trust me, Jen," Hecate insisted. "It won't be that easy."

Jen sighed and rolled her eyes as she left. The only place she could think of to go for a glass jar with a lid was her mother's cabinet, where she kept mason jars for making jellies. Jen god traveled in and out of her mother's kitchen and then went to Morocco and to the Garden of the Hesperides.

As soon as she had arrived, Ladon sensed her. All one hundred heads lifted from where they draped in the branches of Hera's golden apple tree, and all two hundred eyes glared at her. The three nymphs at the base of the tree had been snoring among the huge, gnarly roots, but now they, too, sat up and looked at her.

Jen used the power of Slumber to put them all into the deep boon of sleep. Then she flew up to Ladon—trembling a little at the thought of him suddenly waking up and coiling his hundred necks around her—conjured her sword and pricked the tip into his skin.

All two hundred eyes snapped open.

Without hesitation, Jen god traveled back to Hecate, her heart pounding.

"Did you get it?" Hecate asked.

Jen handed over the empty jar. "Sorry. He woke up."

Hecate quickly took the jar, opened the lid, and collected the single drop sliding down Jen's blade. "This is all I need. Now hold the jar for me while I add the other ingredients."

"What?" Jen laughed with disbelief. "You mean I did it?"

Hecate shook her head with a smile. "I never doubted you for a minute."

Jen really needed to stop doubting herself, too.

The goddess of magic opened her jacket and took out a little silk purse. "This is a pinch of salt." She cinched the sack and returned it to her pocket. Then she took out a small plastic vial. "This is a drop of honey." Then she brought out an apple.

"You carry apples in your pockets?" Jen asked.

Hecate laughed. "I got this while you were gone." She took a bite. "Want some?"

Jen shook her head. "Aren't we in a hurry? We don't have time for a snack."

Hecate broke the apple open and dug out six seeds, which she dropped into the jar. She discarded the rest of the apple. "Now we need a long piece of vine, still green. Let's go cut one from those woods." She pointed to the forest on the island.

Hip found it ironic that the god of slumber was having trouble falling asleep. He'd recently come up with the idea of trying to communicate with Jen in the Dreamworld. The injections of dark magic had made him weak but not sleepy.

It didn't help that the two other gods in the room were drinking wine and talking. Hip noticed that the white god was even slurring his speech. Had he really had enough wine to make him drunk? It then occurred to Hip that the potion might be making him less immune to the effects of the wine. Maybe wine would help Hip sleep.

"Can I have a drink?" Hip asked. "I'm thirsty."

After filling the jar with water from a stream, Hecate put the end of the vine through a hole she had made in the lid.

"Now what?" Jen asked.

"I need to whisper the words of protection from traps and hexes into the jar, and then we'll set it out in the sun. As long as the vine stays green, we'll be protected. But when it turns brown, the spell will lose its power."

Hecate whispered into the jar where the vine came through the hole in the lid. When she had finished her incantation, she wrapped the rest of the vine around the jar, securing it by intertwining it.

"We have about ten minutes, I think," Hecate said. "Let's not waste time."

Jen followed Hecate to the clearing across from Circe's house, half expecting the mountain lions and wolves to attack. Hecate put the jar upright in the sunshine and headed up the path. Jen followed, keeping an eye out for the animals.

When they reached the front door of Circe's angular house, they found it opened. Five wolves stood in a circle in the kitchen, growling. Jen noticed the carcass of the sixth wolf lying on the floor by the hearth, its bones and hide picked clean.

She shuddered, wondering if the other wolves had turned on it, or if it had been eaten after dying of natural causes.

A sudden shriek startled them both. It came from the center of the wolves. Jen thought maybe they had trapped one of the mountain lions.

We don't have time to get involved, Hecate said telepathically. *Grab any bottles you can find.*

Jen flew around the house, trying not to let the pungent odor of dead things get to her, but all of Circe's bottles were lying broken on the white stone floor. Even the open shelving in the kitchen was empty. There was nothing around but broken glass, half-eaten dead things, and growling wolves.

They searched the bedroom, bathroom, and washroom and still found nothing that might be the antidote. Jen flew to the hearth where the black cauldron sat on a heap of ash. The mantle held only one object—a tiny white skull. Jen shuddered.

She flew past the tapestry to the shelves, where she had collected the bottles for Scylla. She knew better than to stand on the trap door, but wondered if the protection spell would protect her from it. Curious about the trap, she lifted the piles of tapestry away from the floor to investigate. Behind the cloth, she found a hidden set of shelves, and on them stood bottles and bottles filled with various colored liquids.

"I hit the mother lode!" she cried to Hecate.

"Jen?" a voice called from the kitchen. It wasn't Hecate's.

The wolves howled.

Jen and Hecate glanced nervously at one another, both still as statues.

"Jen, is that you?" the voice called again. "It's me. Scylla. I need your help!"

When Hip realized he had fallen asleep and was stumbling around in the Dreamworld, he was so excited, that he almost woke himself up. Thank goodness the other gods had been generous with the wine. They'd chuckled when Hip kept begging for more. Metis had even spilled some down the front of Hip's chest as she had held the cup to his lips.

He ran through his dream, through what appeared to be the Fields of Asphodel, but he knew better than that. If he were really in the fields, he wouldn't be running, and Muggie would be lying beside him. He'd also have the power of disintegration, and he didn't.

As if his own subconscious mind were trying to play games with him, he disintegrated into two. He looked at his other self and blinked. Had his powers really been restored?

His other self took off running. Hip followed, calling out, "Wait!"

Now they were in a long corridor. The other Hip turned the corner just up ahead. Hip ran as fast as he could around the corner and saw his other self a few yards away.

"Figment!" Hip shouted. "I command you to show yourself!"

His other self exploded, and left in the wake of the smoke was the eel-like figment, giggling as it flew away.

The ground suddenly crumbled beneath Hip's feet, and he fell into a hole as a surge of water washed over him. Now he was swimming, trying to avoid being sucked out with the current.

"Jen!" he cried, sputtering out the water that had gotten into his mouth. "Jen!"

He grabbed onto a tree root and held on as the water pushed against him. A few yards away, the water fell thousands of feet into a roaring waterfall. Using the root, Hip tried to pull himself from the fast-flowing river. He got one foot onto the bank, and, just when he was about to make it out, the root snapped in half.

He was falling and falling and falling.

Then he heard a voice shout, "You can fly!"

Gliding in the sky across from the waterfall was a butterfly.

Again it shouted, "You can fly!"

Hip realized that, even though he didn't have his godly powers in the Upperworld, where he was trapped on a trick throne, he could fly in the Dreamworld. *Anyone* could fly in the Dreamworld. As the tumultuous river below got closer and closer, Hip pushed off with his toes and soared from the roaring waterfall toward the butterfly.

Now he was running in a meadow of green grass, and he was chasing the butterfly. The scene reminded him of Muggie's dreams. Again, it seemed his own mind wanted to play games with itself, for the butterfly turned into Muggie with wings.

"Muggie?" Hip shouted.

The boy turned and waved.

Of course, it wasn't Muggie, Hip thought. And, aloud he said, "Figment! I command you to show yourself!"

When Muggie did *not* transform into a figment, Hip's mouth dropped open in surprise. Surely this wasn't the *real* Muggie entering Hip's dream. Again, Hip shouted, "Figment! I command you to show yourself!"

The boy only laughed and waved.

Then Hip had an idea. "Wait, Muggie! Can you take me to Jen?"

The boy shrugged and continued to fly, transforming himself into a dragon.

"It's important, son!" Hip had not meant to call the boy *son*. "Tell Jen I'm trapped in northern Siberia, in a gorge between four mountains resembling fingers. Please, Muggie! Can you do that?"

The dragon nodded before it spat fire into the air and sailed away.

Hip had no way of knowing if the boy could really give Jen his message, so he continued to look for her, too.

"Scylla?" Jen said from where she stood near Circe's black cauldron. She glanced at Hecate as they both flew to the kitchen above the growling wolves.

Down in a hole about twenty feet deep, Scylla stood in her beautiful maiden form, looking up at them.

"Scylla?" Hecate glanced once more at Jen before returning her gaze to the pit below. "What are you doing here?"

"My mother told me this body was worthless," Scylla said. "At first, I ran away, but I had nowhere to go. I don't have any friends except for my family."

"You call *them friends*?" Jen asked.

"I know I betrayed you and don't deserve your help, Jen, but I'll tell you something important about the attacks on Gaia if you get me out of here."

Jen crossed her arms. "Why did you come here in the first place?"

"I came looking for the antidote to the beauty potion. I was going to go back to my old self, to please my mother."

"You mean after all the trouble I went through to get you like this…"

"I've had a lot of time down here to think. I've decided to stay as I am. Damn my mother. Damn them all. Maybe I'll go and live among mortals and find friends there."

"We're running out of time," Hecate said. "We need to go."

"My mother's cousin, Metis, is working with Uranus to overthrow Zeus," Scylla said with a voice full of desperation. "They've made promises to my parents in exchange for their support."

"Metis?" Hecate gasped. "I don't believe you."

"And she's pregnant with Zeus's son," Scylla said.

"That's not possible," Hecate said.

"All the gods are sterile, right?" Jen asked Hecate.

"Uranus used Circe's dark magic to make Metis fertile again," Scylla said. "Now please help me!"

Jen disintegrated to look at the vine in the protection charm. It was beginning to turn brown. She filled her bag with all of the potions hidden behind the tapestry.

Then she gave the bag to Hecate. "Take these and go. Hopefully the antidote is there."

"Aren't you coming?" Hecate asked.

"I can't leave Scylla."

"We can come back for her later," Hecate said "I'll make another protection charm."

"I doubt I can fool Ladon a second time."

At that moment, a jolt of electricity shot from the ceiling toward Jen and Hecate. Hecate flew away, begging Jen telepathically to follow. Jen dodged another electric blast as she put the wolves into the deep boon of sleep.

Once she could fully see inside the pit, she groaned. Tree roots had wrapped themselves around Scylla's ankles, preventing her from flying out. Jen conjured her sword again and flew into the pit, hacking away at the roots as electricity continued to attack her. Each time she cut a root in half, it grew twice as long, wrapping around her wrists and neck. Once the tree roots held her captive, she lost her ability to disintegrate. Full of panic, she hacked away as Scylla flew from the pit.

"Thanks!" Scylla said with a cold grin.

As Jen fought the crazy tree roots, she shouted, "You're really going to leave me here?"

"I gave you information, didn't I? We're even now."

Jen grunted when a thick root pinned the hand holding her sword to her leg.

Scylla hovered over the pit as if she might intervene.

"Please, Scylla!" Jen begged. "I know you don't want to be a monster."

"You don't know me at all!" Scylla screamed. "No one knows me!"

"I can't believe I actually thought there was still good in you!" Jen yelled.

"Your foolish gullibility is not my problem!" Scylla flew to Circe's door.

"I really am a fool!" Jen shouted, laughing a low laugh. She couldn't believe she'd trusted that loathsome crab again. Why? Why had she so badly wanted to believe in her?

Like a ton of bricks, the realization hit her. There was a time she'd wanted to believe there was good in her father, too. But toward the end of his life, Jen had given up on him. She hated that she felt guilty for not forgiving him before he died. *She* was the victim. Why should *she* feel guilty? But she did. And she couldn't let it go. And believing in Scylla, forgiving Scylla, finding good in Scylla was her way of dealing with the unresolved guilt she still felt because of her father.

And now that weakness had her trapped in a pit in a witch's lair while her husband's body was about to be possessed by an evil villain wanting to overthrow the Olympians.

She screamed with frustration, her throat burning from the abuse. "I hate myself! I'm such an idiot! Why, Jen? Why are you so stupid!"

<u>CHAPTER TWENTY-THREE</u>

Helpless

They haven't had breakfast yet." Than handed Hermie—still in his P.J.'s and wrapped in a blanket—over to Richard.

"Don't worry about that," Richard said.

Than didn't admit that his kids' breakfast was the last thing on his mind right now. "Thanks."

As Carol took Hestie—bundled up like her brother but still asleep—from Therese's arms, she asked, "Are you sure this is a good idea?"

"We can't wait around and do nothing," Therese said. "We have no idea if the other gods know."

"We'll come home as soon as we can," Than reassured them, though he had no reassurance for himself. All he knew was that his brother was in danger, and there was little he could do about it.

Therese wrapped Aphrodite's traveling robe around the both of them, and they god traveled directly to his parents' palace in the Underworld.

When they entered the main room, they found no one at home. Very rarely did his mother and father leave the palace at the same time, especially without stationing Hecate to stand guard.

"Let's check Tartarus," Than said to Therese. "Maybe my sisters are there."

With a sense of urgency and foreboding, Than followed the winding corridor along the Phlegethon toward Tartarus, holding Therese's hand.

"Tizzie? Meg?" Therese called out into the darkness. "Alecto? Anyone?"

"Pete?" Than cried. "Pete, if you can hear me, please appear."

A pinch in Hip's arm brought him from his dream. He startled awake, forgetting for a moment where he was.

"Well, hello, sunshine," the god said. Then he muttered, "Can you believe my father actually used to say that to me? I might understand Hyperion saying that to *his* son, Helios, but why should my father call *me* sunshine?"

Hip narrowed his eyes at the white god. "So you're Uranus. You took over your father's body."

"It took you long enough." The god made a flame with his hand to sterilize the needle he'd just injected into Hip's arm. "And it's about time, because this, my friend, is our final dose. In four hours, I'll be able to take over *your* body."

"The other gods will not let that happen."

"I can understand your optimism given what Zeus and the other Olympians have already done for you and your family," Uranus said sarcastically. "But since I could not persuade you to consider becoming my ally, I've decided to swallow you as soon as the soul transfer is complete."

"What?" Hip's stomach clenched with nausea. "Then how will you use me as a bargaining chip?"

"I can always eat the herb to regurgitate you, if ever Hades agrees to join my side."

Hip closed his eyes, feeling utterly hopeless and sick. He hadn't been able to find Jen in the Dreamworld and was beginning to doubt that Muggie had been able to deliver his message. To add to his misery, he had a headache from the wine and probably from whatever dark magic was flowing through his system. Why hadn't the other gods found him yet? Was anyone even looking for him?

Jen hadn't been trapped in Circe's pit, entangled in tree roots, for more than a few minutes when she heard a sound in the house above her. At first, she thought it might be Hecate, already coming back for her, but soon she realized it was just the wolves waking from their sleep. Now that she was trapped, the duties of Sleep had probably gone to Hecate. So why hadn't the goddess of the crossroads and magic returned for her?

Expecting the wolves to resume their growling, she was surprised when they whined and ran away. Something must have frightened them, but what?

Then something slithered across the stone wall.

"Hecate?" Jen called.

When a face framed with long black hair and possessing piercing turquoise eyes looked down at her from the opening above, Jen was shocked to realize it belonged to Echidna.

"Well, hello there," the snake woman said.

"What are you doing here?" Jen asked, struggling against the roots to no avail.

"I was looking for my sister, but you're a nice surprise."

"You better get out of here," Jen shouted. "Help is on its way."

"Not in time, I'm sorry to say," Echidna said with a laugh. "I'm hungry, and even though you're a scrawny thing, you'll have to do."

Jen freaked out as Echidna stretched open her mouth wider than Jen thought possible. Jen tugged and pulled and prayed and screamed. "Help!"

"What's going on in here?" came a familiar voice from the doorway. It was Scylla.

Echidna closed her massive mouth and turned toward the door. "Well, hello, sis. You're interrupting my meal."

Echidna whipped her serpent's tail toward Scylla.

"Leave her alone," Scylla said. "Go find some other poor thing to eat."

Jen didn't think she could be any more shocked. Was Scylla actually taking up for her?

"I knew you'd go soft once you got your looks back," Echidna said. "Stay out of this, or I'll eat you next."

"You wouldn't," Scylla said.

"Are you sure about that?" Echidna taunted.

Once again, Echidna stretched her massive mouth wide and leaned over the pit toward Jen. Jen pulled against the roots and screamed and shook her head, willing herself not to be swallowed—one of the worst things that could befall a god. As the slimy forked tongue coiled itself around her, Jen closed her eyes and said goodbye to Hip.

Just when Than was about to suggest that he and Therese god travel to the gates of Mount Olympus and beg to be admitted—which he knew was a risk, since rarely in the ancient history of the gods had mortals ever been permitted in Zeus's palace—Pete appeared in the winding corridor outside of Tartarus.

"Than? Therese? What are you guys doing here?"

"Jen came to us in a dream," Therese said.

"Where's Hip?" Than asked.

Pete's face became grim. "Everyone's out looking for him."

"Is it true that Uranus has him?" Therese asked.

"I'm afraid so." Pete told them what he knew of Uranus's plans.

After Pete had finished, Than felt for the first time since becoming a mortal that he would do anything to take Pete's place. He loved his life with Therese and the twins back in Colorado, but now the entire pantheon was in danger of being overthrown, oppressed, imprisoned, or worse, and he desperately wished he could defend it. In fact, if it wouldn't mean Pete's immediate death, Than would make the trade at this very moment.

"There's got to be something we can do," Than said, as he raked his fingers through his hair.

"Pray," Pete said. "Your prayers give strength to the gods."

Than knew that to be true. He and Therese each embraced Pete before returning home to the Melner Cabin in Colorado, where they sat in their living room and silently prayed.

Hip could tell his godly powers were nearly drained from his body. His acute sense of hearing was gone, his vision was blurred (and was probably worse than that of a mortal), his corporal glow was faint, and, worst of all, he could feel his soul losing its tether to his body.

The potion was having the same effect on Uranus, for the white god sat slumped on the daybed beside Metis and barely moved except to say every few minutes, "It's almost time."

Perhaps because she was bored, Metis crossed the room to Hip and looked down at him affectionately.

"Once this is all over, dear Hypnos, all of our lives will be much improved."

"How can you know that?" he asked her. "Do you have the power of prophecy?"

She smiled and rolled her eyes. They were the same startling gray as Athena's. "No, but I do have wisdom, and I know that it's time for a change. You know it, too. Search your mind and your heart, and you'll find I'm right."

"Zeus has his flaws," Hip said. "But at least we know what we're getting with him. We have no idea what Uranus or your son has in store for the rest of us. What if they mean to send us to Tartarus?"

"I plan to raise my son to love and respect me," she said. "I'll impart my wisdom onto him, and he'll become a great king."

"And what if Athena decides to stand with her father?" Hip asked.

Metis frowned. "Like I said, she has wisdom. She'll know I'm right."

Hip was desperate to get through to Metis while she was no longer under the direct influence of Uranus, who sat quietly on the bed.

"Listen to me, Metis," Hip said. "You were made weak living all those centuries inside of Zeus."

"It was a terrible way to live," she said, anger seeping into her tone.

"And when we freed you, you were confused, remember?"

"Of course. You don't need to speak of it."

"Has it occurred to you that maybe you've been brainwashed?" Hip challenged.

"Metis," Uranus whined. "Stop talking to him and come comfort me. You know this makes me ill."

Metis glared at Hip before turning her back to him and rejoining Uranus on the bed.

Again, Uranus said, "It's almost time."

Just as Echidna's powerful tongue pulled Jen, along with the tree roots and clumps of dirt and rock, from Circe's trap, Echidna's head lobbed at a strange angle, and blood spurt everywhere from her neck. Then Meg sliced Jen free of Echidna's tongue while Tizzy hacked at the tree roots binding her.

A terrible shriek throttled Jen's eardrums. She flew from the pit and was horrified to see Scylla's head fall to the ground. Hecate's blade was stained and dripping with Scylla's blood.

"No!" Jen screamed.

The duties of Sleep called to Jen as she scooped up Scylla's head and body and flew them to the Underworld for safe keeping. Hecate and the Furies followed with a barrage of questions, but Jen couldn't speak through the choking tears.

Finally, she said to them telepathically, *She'd come back to save me from Echidna. She was trying to help me.*

CHAPTER TWENTY-FOUR

Reports

Meg and Tizzie followed Jen to her rooms, where they lay Scylla out on Jen's couch. Even in death, the new goddess was beautiful.

"Are you sure she meant to help you?" Meg moved Scylla's arms to her side and adjusted her hands. "I have a bad feeling about this."

"I'm sure," Jen said as she gently aligned Scylla's neck. "She stood up to Echidna for me."

Jen looked down at Scylla's face, trying to forget the monster to remember the good. She held back the tears, but the guilt she felt over what had happened plagued her. Why did it feel like her father was dying all over again?

Tizzie covered Scylla's body with a sheet of silk. "Could it have been a trick?"

Jen shook her head. "No. I don't think so."

"We're taking a risk bringing her here," Meg pointed out. "When she recovers, she could attack us."

"We should bind her with adamantine chains, just in case," Tizzie suggested. "And we should interrogate her soul in Tartarus."

"I don't know," Jen said. She didn't want Scylla to think she'd been betrayed by Jen and taken as a prisoner of the Underworld. "Is that really necessary?"

"Better safe than sorry," Meg said.

While Jen watched Meg and Tizzie bind Scylla's body, she also accompanied Hecate to Mount Olympus, to tell the other gods what Scylla had told them about Metis.

"This must be his ace in the hole," Poseidon exclaimed beside his prisoner, still encased in the golden net.

Hera's mouth dropped open, and she turned an angry gaze toward Zeus. "You slept with Metis?"

"Not intentionally, dear. I was tricked!"

"Nevertheless," Hades interrupted. "We have Prometheus's prophecy to contend with."

Jen wondered what Hades thought of Zeus being on the other side of his own dirty work. Zeus had once disguised himself as Hades so that he could trick Persephone into lying with him. It was how Melinoe had been conceived.

"Can you see anything?" Aphrodite asked Apollo.

"No," Apollo admitted. "But I'll keep trying. And I'll be sure to report all of my visions, as soon as they happen."

"We need to find Prometheus and question him," Zeus said.

"No one has seen him for centuries," Aphrodite pointed out.

Hera continued to stew angrily, her mouth in a straight line, her arms crossed at her chest. She had not taken the news about Metis well, but she seemed less worried about being overthrown than she was about Zeus's infidelity—however accidental it may have been.

"My son is my priority at the moment," Hades said. "Excuse me while I return to the search."

Hades disappeared.

"Jen Holt," Poseidon said, pulling her from her thoughts. "How is it going in Siberia? Are there any leads?"

While Jen had been reporting her news on Mount Olympus and laying out the body of Scylla in her room in the Underworld, she'd also been scanning the cold mountains of northern Siberia with some of the other Olympians. Hestia, Artemis, and Athena searched the valleys and gorges on foot while Jen, Persephone, Hephaestus, and Hermes combed the peaks and mountainsides from the air. Ares flew through the upper sky in his chariot, questioning the cloud nymphs.

Just as Poseidon was asking Jen his question about leads, a Giant leapt from its hiding place and pinned Athena to the ground with one of its claws.

"We're under attack!' Jen said to Poseidon. "Another Giant. He's trapped Athena!"

All of the gods in the area converged on the Giant. As Jen neared the beast, she noticed that every one of its sockets was empty and bloody, and a spear stuck up between the red spikes in its back. Although it was blind, the monster had no trouble smelling its enemies as they surrounded it. All three heads shrieked ear-shattering screeches and spat streaks of fire, while simultaneously swatting at the gods with that tail of iron.

Artemis avoided the attacking flames and shot arrow after arrow at the Giant's underbelly. Hephaestus threw one ax after another down on the Giant's back, barely dodging its ferocious tail. Jen snuck to one of the last of the Giant's hundred feet and thrust her sword between two of its back claws. The monster screamed in pain as Jen god traveled to a nearby rock.

Ares shot out of the sky in his chariot, plummeted toward the beast, and lodged a spear right between the eyes of the center head. The head fell forward, and the entire beast wobbled unsteadily. Hephaestus moved in and cut clean through the neck. The claw pinning Athena lifted as the beast flailed to regain its balance. The severed head rolled down the mountainside. Hestia flew beneath the beast and rescued Athena. Then Persephone drove her spear through one of the sockets of the remaining heads.

As Jen flew back to continue with the fight, she was alarmed by something Muggie was telling her in the Dreamworld. She'd gone to his dream for comfort, even though she also lay curled up with him in the Asphodel, and they'd been sliding down the rainbow arch with Iris (or a figment appearing as Iris); but, now he was tugging at her hand and saying again and again, "He's in the gorge between four fingers! The gorge between four fingers!"

In Siberia, Jen leapt into the air and flew above the mountain range. Down below, she spotted four slender peaks that towered above the other formations in the area. They looked like human fingers! As she flew in their direction, she telepathically reported the news to all the other gods in her reach.

I think I know where Hip is! Muggie found me in the Dreamworld and delivered a message from him. He's in the gorge between four fingers. I'm flying there now!

Wait! Many of the gods replied simultaneously.

Don't charge in without a plan! Athena warned.

We might not have time to wait! Jen replied.

Hades overtook her in his chariot and said, "Get in!"

As Ares, Hermes, and Hephaestus finished off the Giant in Siberia, the other gods reconvened on Mount Olympus to quickly discuss a plan. It took every ounce of Jen's self-control not to rush into the gorge and search for Hip. Would the other gods know if she sneaked around on her own? What was preventing her from disintegrating and returning to Siberia to investigate the gorge? Nothing.

So she did just that.

In the great hall of Mount Olympus, Hades turned to her and said, "If you must go, take my helm."

Beneath the helm of invisibility, Jen descended into the icy gorge between the four peaks resembling fingers. She reached out telepathically to Hip but received no reply.

Hundreds of feet into the gorge, near the very bottom, Jen spotted the entrance to a cave and noticed a thin line of smoke coming from it, disappearing in the blustery snow. She flew to the entrance and peered inside.

She covered her mouth to stop the gasp from escaping her lips at the site of Hip bound on a golden chair. His eyes were closed, his skin pale. He looked like he was dead. Across from him on a sofa bed were two other gods. She recognized Metis and assumed the other must be Uranus in Aether's body. His long white hair fell around his shoulders and his chrome eyes were hooded.

"It's time," the god said. "Help me, Metis."

"Don't do this!" Hip suddenly opened his eyes.

Jen's heart was breaking, her head was in a state of confusion, and her heart was clambering up to her throat. It was now or never, she told herself. She had to *think* and to *do* something fast.

Back on Mount Olympus, she interrupted the other gods to report what she saw. "Hip's chained to a golden chair. He's weak. So is Uranus. Metis is there helping him. He said it's time! We have to do something now! Uranus is going to possess Hip's body!"

"The golden chair is the trick throne Hephaestus made for Hera a long time ago," Aether said from the golden net. "Uranus took it when Hera tossed it down from Mount Olympus."

"That horrible thing is still around?" Hera glared at the other gods, as if she was daring them to blame her for Hip being trapped.

"Send Hephaestus now to release Hypnos before it's too late," Aether urged them.

"Hermes is too far away for me to summon," Zeus said. "He's still out in Siberia."

"Jen!" Persephone cried.

"I'm on it!" she said as she disintegrated again and dispatched to northern Siberia.

"Give Hephaestus my helm!" Hades told her.

Jen left the gorge between the four fingers to deliver the helm to Hephaestus. She quickly explained what he needed to do.

"I need the key," Hephaestus said. "And I don't know where it is."

CHAPTER TWENTY-FIVE

Last Chances

What do you mean you don't know where it is?" Jen asked Hephaestus anxiously. "It's our only hope of rescuing Hip!"

"It's been eons since I used that chair," he said.

They god traveled to Mount Olympus while Jen took the helm and went back to the cave to check on Hip.

In the cave, Uranus was on his knees before the trick throne, holding hands with Hip. He was chanting, "Transfer my soul into his vessel and his soul into mine. Do not permit Death to wrestle either soul from either vessel at this time. As I take possession of his body, and he does the same to mine, protect us from Death and the collectors of ghouls so that I become his and he mine."

Jen watched on with horror, unable to breathe. Uranus began to repeat his chant. Hip just sat there slumped on the throne looking as dead as Scylla.

On Mount Olympus, Hecate was performing magic of her own. She wrote "the key to Hephaestus's trick throne" on a slip of paper and set it in a silver bowl. She added a pinch of salt and a drop of honey and then set the paper on fire.

"Wait for the paper to burn completely," she said to the other gods who had crowded around to watch. "Once the paper is ash and there are no more embers, we can follow the smoke to the lost object."

"Please hurry!" Jen begged. "Uranus is performing his ritual right now!"

Back in the Fields of Asphodel, Jen clung to Muggie and allowed her tears to flow uninhibited. She wailed and moaned, knowing she wouldn't wake the sleeping child from his slumber. In the Dreamworld, she stopped sliding down rainbows and lay on the grass and beat the ground. She'd never felt so frightened and helpless. She couldn't let Uranus trap Hip's soul and steal Hip's godly powers! But what could she do?

"Jen?"

She sat up in the grass in the Dreamworld and saw Hip walking toward her.

She knew it was just a figment, but she needed to hold him so badly. She got up and ran to him and held him tight.

"Even if your soul is ripped from your body, I'll find a way to save you!" she said.

"Uranus plans to swallow me once he's transferred me into his father's body," he said. "I've come to tell you goodbye, just in case I never make it out again."

Jen did not like the way her dream was going. "Figment, I command you to show yourself!"

When Hip gazed down at her with eyes full of sadness and despair, she threw her arms around his neck and sobbed against him.

"I'll love you forever!" she cried. "I'll never stop! No matter what!"

Back on Mount Olympus, Jen could not control her trembling hands and quaking limbs as she and the other gods waited for the slip of paper to burn into ash. Her teeth chattered as she watched anxiously for the embers to die out. Then all the gods lifted their heads as the white smoke curled in the air above them and floated through the hall toward Hermes's throne.

Hermes rushed to the base of his chair, popped open a compartment, and lifted the key in the air. Then he gave it to Hephaestus, who immediately god traveled to the gorge where Jen was waiting with the helm.

Jen hovered by a snow drift outside the granite cave while Hephaestus entered beneath the protection of the helm. She held her breath and prayed harder than she ever had before.

The other gods had gathered in the gorge as silently as the snowflakes that fell from above, where the cloud nymphs looked down, as anxious as the rest. Jen glanced at all their worried faces and was glad they were there to keep her company during the agonizing wait.

I've got Hypnos! Hephaestus prayed to all the gods, which was all they needed to send them into the cave.

As Jen followed Hephaestus back to Mount Olympus, she also stood inside the cave and, with the other gods, charged toward Uranus and Metis. Metis disappeared in a flash. Jen tried to follow, but she lost the scent of the goddess and had no idea which way she'd gone.

Uranus was weak as Athena and Artemis took each of his arms and they all returned to Mount Olympus.

Than had been gripping Therese's hand on their living room couch, deep in prayer, when his mother appeared to them.

"Hypnos has been found," she said.

Than jumped to his feet, relief sweeping over him. "Is he hurt?"

Therese stood beside him. "Is he going to be okay?"

Persephone put a hand on each of their shoulders. "He's weak, but Hecate found an antidote to the black magic Uranus was using on him, and Apollo is helping him to recover."

"Can we see him?" Than asked.

Persephone dropped her hands and began to wring them. "I don't know if that's a good idea."

Therese gave Than a worried glance. "Why not?"

Metis was working with Uranus, and she got away. It's still too dangerous. I don't want you two caught in the crossfire.

"Surely we'll be safe in the Underworld," Than objected.

"It's unpleasant there at the moment," Persephone said. "Your sisters are interrogating Uranus in Tartarus. You can hear them throughout the entire realm."

Hip woke up with a bitter taste in his mouth, and his head still felt like it was in a vice. He glanced down and was relieved to see he was in his own body. He was lying on Apollo's couch, and Jen was sitting on a pillow on the floor with her face close to his, her hands holding his.

"Hey, there, handsome," Jen said with a smile. Tears had flooded her eyes.

"Hey, there, beautiful."

"How do you feel?"

He felt like crap, but what he said was, "Happy."

Jen touched her lips to his and whispered, "Me, too."

"So, tell me what happened? Is Uranus caught?"

"Pete took his soul to Tartarus, along with Aether's, and the Furies are interrogating them."

Hip shuddered. He could only imagine his sisters' wrathful vengeance. "What about Metis?"

Jen bit her lip. "She got away. The others are searching for her."

"Oh, no." He laid back his head and closed his eyes. "Did you know that she's…"

"Pregnant."

"Circe and her dark magic," Hip moaned. "We should have burned her house down after we threw her in Tartarus."

"Maybe," Jen said. "But then Scylla wouldn't have gotten her second chance."

Hip wasn't sure he agreed with Jen, though now wasn't the time to say so. Instead, he asked, "How's Muggie?"

"Anxious to see you." Jen reached out and combed his hair out of his eyes. "Should I step out for a moment so he can come in? He's waiting with Hecate."

"Okay."

Jen kissed him once more before she disappeared. It occurred to Hip that she was getting more and more comfortable with the whole goddess thing.

When Muggie ran into the room and threw himself across Hip's chest, Hip busted out laughing.

"I'm so happy to see you, little man!" Hip mussed the little boy's black curls. "How you doin'?"

Muggie lifted his smiling face to Hip. "Is jy my pappa?"

Although Hip hesitated for a moment, having been caught off guard by the question, he knew the answer and grinned. "Ja, my seun. Ek is jou pappa."

Jen watched the exchange between Hip and Muggie, holding back tears. She hoped Zeus would honor the promise he'd made, or he'd have hell to pay. Jen wasn't about to see her fledgling family hurt.

As she watched her boys, she disintegrated and went looking for Scylla, who was staying in one of her rooms near the asphodel. Scylla was sitting at a small table eating a bowl of strawberries and drinking ambrosia when Jen entered.

"We never eat like this at home," the new goddess said. "This is delicious."

"There's more where that came from."

The corners of Scylla's mouth quirked. "I suppose being good has its perks."

Jen studied the other goddess, wondering if she was sincere. "There's a place for you with the Olympians, if you want it."

Scylla kept her eyes on the bowl of strawberries. "I have no purpose, Jen."

Jen sat at the small table across from her. "Why can't you be the guide for lost sailors? Instead of challenging them, you can help them find their way."

The other goddess glanced sharply at Jen, like a deer in the beam of headlights. Then she said, "I have to admit that my new palate much prefers fruit to human flesh."

Jen cracked a smile.

But then Scylla frowned.

"What is it?" Jen leaned forward.

Scylla met Jen's gaze. "What if I can't do this? What if I'm not meant to be good?"

Jen reached across the table to take Scylla's hand. She hesitated in touching her, afraid of rejection, or of retaliation, of the evil frothing just below the surface, but Jen fought the fear and took the hand anyway. "I truly believe that we can choose our destinies."

"The Fates are never wrong."

"But they don't choose for us. They just see ahead of time the choices we'll make."

"How do you know that?"

Jen squeezed Scylla's hand and let go. "It's what I believe. It's what my mother always said. She'd say, with a cigarette in one hand and a cup of black coffee in the other, 'You're the captain of your own ship, baby doll.'" Jen tried to copy her mother's voice.

They both laughed at Jen's silly imitation.

"I hope she's right," Scylla said.

"She usually is."

"You're lucky, to have such a mother." Scylla frowned and seemed to turn in to herself.

Jen reached out her hand to squeeze Scylla's once more. "I know. But I had a monster living with me, too. Luckily my mom and Pete, they watched out for me."

"I don't have that," Scylla said. "My dad and siblings couldn't care less."

Jen cocked her head to one side. She still wasn't sure if she could completely trust the new goddess. Her words could be another form of manipulation. After a beat, she sighed, thinking she'd rather err on the side of compassion than suspicion. Jen felt sorry for Scylla and didn't want her to feel like she was alone in the world. "You have me."

As soon as the duties of Sleep returned to Hip, he helped with the search for Metis. During the interrogation by the Furies in Tartarus, Uranus had admitted that he and Metis had rebuilt Cronos's palace on Mount Othrys. The gods—including Athena, who'd been devastated by the news about her mother—had searched the ancient castle but had found no trace of Metis there. So they set up a watch rotation and continued to search the area.

After days of searching, the gods were summoned by Zeus to a meeting on Mount Olympus. Jen and Hip stood with the other Underworld gods near Hades and his throne. The only Olympians not present were Demeter and Dionysus. Most of the others were there, including their children. Ariadne and Asterion, Eros and Psyche, all of the Muses and Charities, and Cybele and her Curetes were among them. The great hall was crowded and loud and boisterous.

Once everyone who was coming had arrived and was in their places in the hall, Zeus asked for silence.

The voices hushed, and the room became quiet.

Zeus stood up before his throne so all could see him. "A day may come, perhaps ten or twenty years from now, when you will need to make a decision."

Hip glanced at Jen. *I wonder what this is about.*

"An ancient prophecy from Prometheus claims that a son born to me by Metis will one day overthrow me."

Chatter erupted in the hall but died down when Zeus raised his hands for silence.

"As many of you already know, Uranus used dark magic to make Metis fertile, and then Metis tricked me into lying with her."

Hera's face turned as red as a pomegranate.

"I know I've made many mistakes during my reign, some of which are unforgiveable." Zeus glanced at Hades and Persephone. Hip wondered if Zeus had ever asked for their forgiveness. Zeus's eyes then fell on Hera, who did not return his gaze. "In spite of my flaws and imperfections, I've tried to be a good leader, though I know I have failed many times over."

Hip was moved when Zeus's eyes beseeched his own.

"Uranus has already shown that he will support my son," Zeus continued. "He wants to help him form a new reigning pantheon, which may or may not include all of you."

Hip noticed Poseidon looking suspiciously at Athena, and Ares studied Hades in the same vein. Were they already breaking apart, just by the thought of a rebellion? Would the gods become so suspicious of one another that they wouldn't need the threat if Uranus to bring down the pantheon?

"So, each of you must think on this. Do you want to stand with Uranus, Metis, and her son, and the others who surely hate me and want to see me overthrown? Or do you want to stand beside me, even though it may end in defeat?"

"This prophecy didn't come from the Fates," Athena, sitting on Zeus's right, interrupted. "It may never come to be."

Zeus shrugged. "Perhaps. At any rate, we have no way of knowing when my son will be born or when or if he will begin to turn on me. No one needs to declare his or her loyalty just yet. But do know this: Though I am far from perfect, as a sign of my sincere regret for the crimes I've committed against my wife, I hereby swear on the River Styx that I will never knowingly be unfaithful to my beautiful Hera again."

Hera finally returned his gaze with a hint of a smile on her face.

Zeus continued, "And I promise all of you that I will do everything in my power to serve each and every one of you as your leader. None of us is born with all the answers. None of us is born perfect. Over time we learn from our mistakes. I have made more mistakes than anyone here, so it stands to reason that I have also learned the most."

A few people dared to laugh, but Zeus did not admonish them. Instead, he smiled. "Choose to follow me, to defend our reigning pantheon, and I will do everything in my power to protect you."

Applause erupted in the palace.

Aphrodite cried, "Hear, hear!"

Hip glanced around at the faces of the Olympians and found most of them were smiling back at Zeus. Hip glanced at his father, standing beside him, but couldn't read his expression. Hades was neither smiling nor frowning. As a chill ran down his back, Hip wondered if the lord of the Underworld would one day rule a new establishment.

As if Zeus were wondering the same thing, he lifted his arms to quiet the crowd and added, "As a goodwill sign of my sincere and deep regret for having committed sins against Hades and his family, I hereby condemn myself to take over the annual punishment by the Maenads, which Thanatos previously suffered for breaking an oath."

Gasps filled the great hall. Hip felt his mouth drop open as Jen sought his gaze with her own. Once again, her eyes had filled with tears of happiness. Hip had to admit that this was a smart move for Zeus.

Zeus locked eyes with Hades, as though he expected a response of some kind. Hip watched his father anxiously. Hades made no comment, but he gave Zeus a nod of thanks, and—miracle of miracles—a smile. It was subtle, and it disappeared so quickly, that Hip wondered if he had imagined it.

The crowd erupted again with chatter and laughter until Zeus once more raised his hands for silence.

"I have one more announcement," Zeus said. "As another sign to you that my word is honorable, we shall end this gathering with a celebration."

Hip glanced again around the room, noting the definite change of mood among the Underworld gods and some of the others, who might have been on the fence about supporting Zeus. Then he heard Zeus call his name, and he looked again at his king.

"Weeks ago, we made a promise to one another," Zeus said. "And you fulfilled your end of our deal. Now it is time that I fulfill mine."

<u>CHAPTER TWENTY-SIX</u>

Morpheus

Hip was in awe, as, in less than an hour, the Charities had decorated the great hall with flowers, the muses had set up a small orchestra, and Hestia, with the help of a few sea nymphs, had laid out food on banquet tables in the dining hall. Demeter had been brought from her winter cabin. Dionysus (who later admitted that he was the one who had stolen the key to Hephaestus's trick throne and had hidden it in Hermes's secret compartment) had been summoned from Mount Kithairon. The Furies had taken Hades's chariot and had picked up Bobby and Mrs. Stern, along with Therese, Than, and their twins, and had brought them to Mount Olympus to join the party. Even Clifford got to come along for the ride, though he decided to visit Cubie and Galen in the Underworld rather than join the party on Mount Olympus.

Hecate, who rarely thought of herself, had volunteered to take over the duties of Sleep, so that the mortals could be present in the same room with Hip without passing out. Hecate had delivered Muggie to Hip, and after he kissed her cheek and thanked her repeatedly, the goddess of magic and the crossroads left. Muggie yawned and stretched in Hip's arms as Jen bent over to kiss his forehead. When he opened his eyes, he had the cutest, sweetest smile on his face.

"Mama and Pappa!" the boy said—his new names for Jen and Hip.

Hip's heart felt as though it could burst, it was so full.

Jen laughed a huge belly laugh—which she hadn't done in ages, it seemed. Her mom and Bobby had never been to Mount Olympus, and their chins couldn't be any closer to the floor. Luckily, Ares found them and gave them a personal tour and put them both at ease.

Jen noticed Meg give Bobby a wink and say, "You've grown since I last saw you!" Then the Fury turned to Tizzie and said, "Yummy!"

Jen thought she would faint with laughter as Bobby's ears turned bright pink.

Jen was also excited to have Scylla among the gods and goddesses in the great hall. The ex-monster wasn't the bubbliest personality, and Jen made a note that she'd have to work with her on her people skills. But at least Scylla was there, making an effort, after having sworn on the River Styx to Tizzie and Meg that she meant no harm. She seemed more content after Jen had told some of the others about Scylla's new purpose: the goddess of lost sailors. From now on, instead of *eating* sailors, she would help them find their way. Jen crossed her fingers that Scylla wouldn't go back to her old ways the first time she came across a plump young sea captain.

It was also amazingly excellent to have her best friends, Therese and Than, with her on this special day. The twins looked adorable—Hestie in her yellow dress and pigtails and Hermie in his black suit and shiny black shoes. Their eyes were wide as they took in their surroundings with awe.

Jen could also tell that all of the other gods were more at ease now that Uranus had been officially banned to Tartarus. Aether, having been restored to his own body with Hecate's help, had been released on good faith, but the other gods would be keeping an eye on him, just in case. Jen believed that the god of the upper air had proven his trustworthiness when he had told them all about the trick throne. That piece of information had surely saved them all.

Best of all, her two boys looked handsome—Hip standing beside her in his white shirt and blue trousers with Muggie in his arms, wearing his new clothes and shoes. Jen couldn't imagine a happier ending to this incredible day than to see their sweet boy turned into a god.

Jen noticed a large golden bowl was being brought into the center of the hall by Hebe—Zeus and Hera's daughter and the goddess of play. Zeus stood before his throne and lifted his arms high in the air, calling for silence. The muses stopped playing their instruments and singing their song. The other gods and goddesses stopped eating and drinking and talking. And everyone looked toward the center of the room where Zeus was heading—toward the golden bowl.

Zeus beckoned to Jen and Hip. "Bring the boy forward."

Hip didn't know why he was nervous as he stepped to the center of the room with Muggie in his arms and Jen at his side. Maybe it was because everyone was looking at him.

Before Zeus spoke again, he put a hand on Hip's head and said, tele-pathically, *Mnemosyne has come to restore your memories. I want you to have them before we continue. And if, once they've returned to you, you still believe it was the right decision, she will do the same for your siblings. Do you accept this plan?*

Hip suddenly felt tongue-tied, not having expected his memories would be returned today. He nodded, though, because he was anxious to have them back.

Mnemosyne, the mother of the Muses and goddess of memory, stepped forward. She dipped her hands into the bowl, which was full of ambrosia. She blessed it and anointed his head.

For a moment, Hip was dizzy, as a whirlwind of images rushed to his mind. In a matter of minutes, he could see with perfect clarity the day of his birth on the island of Delos, the struggle with Hera, the help from Hecate and Dione, and eventually Artemis when the Harpies attacked. He also saw his mother and father happy and in love. And he saw the tenderness they showed him—the rides on Cerberus with this brother, the frog races, the dinner with the pig farmer in the Upperworld, the Trojan War and his sisters and brother bringing blessing to the soldiers.

As his eyes filled with tears, Hip turned to his parents. His heart was now filled with both sorrow and joy, but he was happy to know the truth. He understood his family with greater clarity. Most of all, he understood why his father had become distant and hard.

When his mother gave him a questioning look, Hip closed his eyes and nodded. Tears slipped down his cheeks, but he didn't care. Jen put an arm around him and kissed his ear, asking telepathically if he was okay. He nodded again as everyone in the room continued to watch in silence.

Zeus once again addressed the crowd. "Hypnos has just received his childhood memories."

Gasps filled the room and many mouths fell open as the eyes of those present searched Hip's face for his reaction.

Zeus continued. "His memories were erased for his benefit many years ago. The belief at the time was that the comparison between his early childhood and what followed would be too heartbreaking to endure."

Hip glanced at Than and his sisters, noticing the confused looks on their faces. Were they coming to realize that they, too, had lost their earliest memories?

If they had been wondering it, Zeus confirmed their suspicions when he said, "The same was done to his siblings—all except Melinoe, who, unfortunately, chose not to join us today." Zeus frowned.

Hip noticed his sisters exchange glances of surprise. Than met Hip's gaze with a pale face.

"However," Zeus continued, "with Hip's recommendation, Mnemosyne will now return their memories, too, if they want them. Thanatos? Alecto? Tisiphone? Megaera? If you wish to have your childhood memories restored, please step forward."

Hip told his siblings telepathically that he highly recommended it. *It's amazing, guys. And I love you all so much.*

One by one, Hip's siblings came to the center near the golden bowl of ambrosia. Hip could tell they were in shock and felt somewhat hesitant. Again, he reassured them through prayer that they wouldn't be sorry.

Thanatos glanced back at Therese, who gave him a reassuring nod as he stepped to the center of the great hall. It was funny, because he hadn't thought he would ever set foot in this place again, and now here was another unexpected surprise. He was about to discover a part of himself that he'd never known existed.

He noticed Meg's hands were trembling and Tizzie's hair occasionally hissed as they circled the golden bowl. Even Alecto looked nervous, her red hair appearing to be just on the brink of flames.

Mnemosyne dipped her fingers into the bowl of ambrosia and anointed each of their foreheads. As soon as he'd been touched by the goddess, the images of his past assaulted him. He saw his brother's birth, the wave of protection being shattered and nearly drowning him and Hip. He felt the Harpies and heard their terrifying screams. He remembered playing in Demeter's rooms—running and jumping all over the walls. He remembered taking rides on Cerberus, feeding the Hydra, taming the snakes, and racing pigs and, later, frogs. He remembered bringing life and merriment with his brother to the wounded soldiers during the Trojan War. Most of all, he remembered that his parents had been happy.

Persephone embraced Than and did the same to her other children. "Are you okay?" she asked them.

The Furies nodded, though they didn't speak, or at least, not aloud where he could hear them. Perhaps they each had silent prayers for their parents.

Than kissed his mother's cheek. Then he did something he'd never done before. He put his arms around his father and kissed his cheek, too.

When he caught his father's expression, Than noticed a tear in the corner of his eye. Than quickly looked away, unable to bear it. The last thing he needed was to break down before this enormous crowd. Instead, he glanced around the room to see all the gods and goddesses wiping their eyes, covering their mouths, and otherwise rejoicing at this happy moment of enlightenment.

Therese moved beside him and squeezed his arm. She had no idea what he was remembering. He looked forward to sharing his earliest memories with her once they were home in Colorado.

Colorado. It seemed so far away to Than at the moment. Being surrounded by nearly all of the gods on Mount Olympus was something that had rarely happened in his life. It had happened when he was a young boy—and he was only now remembering it. And it had happened after Therese had come into his life. Therese had helped the Underworld gods to become more accepted by the other Olympians, but before he'd had much opportunity to experience their acceptance and, in some cases, fondness, he'd given it all up to join Therese as a mortal.

He took in a slow breath, trying to enjoy this moment, hoping the memory would last him for the rest of his mortal life.

Zeus lifted his hands in the air and asked for everyone's attention. "Now it is time to confer the gift of immortality on this child that Jen and Hypnos have taken as their own."

Therese avoided Than's eyes as she watched the ceremony, feeling both happy for her friends and jealous for herself. Why couldn't she be happy with her life just as it was? It was a brilliant, amazing, incredible life that anyone would be grateful to have. So why was she watching her best friend with a gut full of envy?

Zeus dipped a cup into the golden bowl and offered the ambrosia to Muggie.

"Drink the food of the gods, so that you may be one of us," Zeus said.

Muggie took the cup and looked first at Jen and then at Hip, who nodded his encouragement. Then the boy put the cup to his lips and drank.

After his first sip, Muggie made a funny face—as though he hadn't expected it to taste so sweet. This caused many of those present to chuckle. Then Muggie licked his lips and nodded before drinking down the rest.

As the boy finished off the last of the ambrosia, Zeus said, "From henceforth, you shall be the god of Dreams and you will be known as Morpheus."

Muggie—or Morpheus—handed the empty cup to Jen, who passed it over to Hebe. Everyone in the room watched in utter silence as the boy's dark skin took on a luminous sheen, like shiny bronze. Then his black eyes became ringed with silver, and silver wings sprouted from his back. His mouth dropped open with surprise as he jumped from Hip's arms and tried out the wings.

Morpheus twirled and flittered above them with a huge grin on his face. He turned somersaults and back flips and spun like the propellers of a helicopter.

Then Iris flew down from her rainbow and joined Morpheus in his graceful air dance.

Therese was happy—truly happy—for Jen and her new family, but the miracle she'd just witnessed made her that much more determined to find a miracle of her own one day.

Morpheus, Jen thought, watching her son—her *son*—flying overhead with Iris. Morpheus was the perfect name for her son. Hip had called him a chameleon because of the easy way the boy had transformed from one thing to another in the Dreamworld. As she watched her little Morpheus trying out his new wings in the space above them in the great hall, she squeezed Hip's hand.

Bobby caught her gaze from across the room and gave her a nod that said, "I told you so."

Jen laughed and leapt up to dance in the air with Morpheus and Iris. Soon Pete and Tizzie joined in, too. Jen heard her mother's hee-haw laughter, and it filled her with happiness. Then Hip came up and wrapped his arms around her waist. Her heart nearly burst with joy.

The muses resumed their music, and the other gods joined in the dancing—some on the floor and others in the air. Persephone flew up with a wreath of spring flowers and set it on Morpheus's dark curls.

"Welcome to the family," she said.

Jen glanced down at Hades. The Underworld gods sometimes referred to him as the gatekeeper, and, at the moment, the gatekeeper looked plenty happy, too.

After the party, Hip took his wife and son on a trip in his father's chariot. First they dropped off their family members in Colorado and hugged them all goodbye. Morpheus was especially excited to learn that he now had cousins, and he asked if he would see them again.

"Soon," Hip assured him.

Little Hestie and Hermie waved goodbye and blew their kisses as Hip turned the chariot back up into the night sky.

Before Morpheus would begin his training in the Dreamworld, Hip wanted to show him the Upperworld. He taught him the names of the lands and oceans, which the boy could keenly see with his godly vision. Hip introduced him to Selene on one side of the globe and to Helios on the other. He showed him Poseidon's palace beneath the Aegean. He pointed out Phorcys's castle in the Ionian Sea, warning him to avoid those waters and the monsters in the surrounding area. He showed Morpheus the seven wonders of the world and introduced him to some of the Nephelae and other water nymphs. Morpheus begged to climb one of Iris's rainbows, so they did it, with the goddess's permission, as a family.

Hip showed his son the monkeys of South America, the giraffes and elephants of the African Savannah, the great bears of Asia, and the penguins and sea lions in the Arctic. While near the North Pole, Hip pointed out the amazing lights from the aurora borealis. Morpheus watched on, as he had everything he'd been shown, with awe and wonder.

Epilogue

Jen had taken Morpheus to celebrate the holidays at Carol and Richard's house, where Therese and Than, their twins, and Jen's mom and stepdad and Bobby had all gathered. Even Ares had come for a short time, and the two Cardinals had a special place on the decorated tree.

After the food and the exchange of gifts and the surprise visit from Santa Claus (Mr. Stern in a wig and beard), Jen and Morpheus said their goodbyes and flew home to Hip. They hadn't been there long when Hades called them to his chambers.

Apollo was there with him, and the expression on his face was grim.

"We'd better sit down," Persephone said.

They gathered around the golden table where they sometimes shared a family meal and waited for Apollo to begin.

"As I've already mentioned to Hades, I've had a vision," Apollo said.

"It concerns Thanatos's twins," Hades said.

"What?" Hip asked.

"What did you see?" Jen asked anxiously.

"I can't see why or how yet," Apollo said, "but I see Hermie and Hestie with Prometheus."

"When?" Hip asked.

"The twins look to be about sixteen or seventeen mortal years old," Apollo replied.

"Why are they with Prometheus?" Jen asked. "Isn't he an enemy to Zeus?"

"I don't know," Apollo said. "I've not mentioned this vision to anyone else, for fear of putting your family in danger, but if Zeus asks, I will have to tell him."

Morpheus cupped Jen's cheek and turned her gaze to meet his. "What's wrong. Mamma?"

"Don't worry, my sweet," she said with a forced smile. "Everything will be okay."

THE END

Thank you for reading my story. I hope you enjoyed it! If you did, please consider leaving a review. Reviews help authors get discovered by more readers.

Please enjoy the first chapter of the next book, *Hunting Prometheus*.

Secrets Revealed

After Therese had blown out her candles and had opened the presents of her favorite bath and body products from her aunt and uncle and Mr. and Mrs. Stern, she went outside to the two giant Elms in the back of what was now her aunt and uncle's property, searching for her favorite red birds—her parents. She couldn't understand their song without the help of Hermie and Hestie to translate, but she had a feeling they were singing her a happy birthday wish. Besides, their words were less important than their presence. Their gift of immortality—even if they couldn't be human—had been the best gift anyone had ever given her.

And she had received many amazing gifts, she thought, as she clutched the lockets around her neck. One had come from Athena, with the inscription: "The most common way people give up their power is by believing they have none." The other had been a Christmas present from her Aunt Carol, and it contained a photo of her parents on one side and a photo of Carol, Richard, and Lynn on the other. She rarely took the lockets off.

She'd also received a crown of invisibility from Artemis. It wasn't as powerful as Hades's helm. The crown could only hide one from mortals. But it had come in handy over the years, especially when Jen had still lived at home.

Perhaps the most useful was the traveling robe from Aphrodite. The first one had been ripped to shreds years ago, during Therese's challenge with the Hydra, but Aphrodite had given her another one after the twins were born. It had helped Therese get around when she was in a hurry, and it had also helped her to take Than and the twins to visit the Underworld from time to time—though it had been almost a year since they'd been. She would go more often if she didn't feel as though she was in the way. The gods were busy and rarely seemed to have time for Therese and her family.

And of course, her animal companions—Clifford, Jewels, and Stormy—had been granted immortality, which had been a wonderful thing; though, she had to admit it only reminded her of what she and Than had lost. Now *Jen* road Stormy across the skies, and Therese rarely saw him. And she worried about who would take care of Clifford and Jewels once Therese and Than and the twins were in the Elysian Fields of the Underworld, living eternity in blissful oblivion.

She blinked away her tears. Thirty-seven. She was thirty-seven years old. She and Than had both aged and were reminded of it every time they saw the ever-youthful Hip and Jen, Pete and Tizzie, and the others. In fact, Therese now looked the same age as Persephone, and Than looked more like Hades's brother than his son. Maybe that was another reason they didn't visit the Underworld often.

She was brought from her reverie when she heard the twins around the corner on the deck at the side of the house. They seemed unaware of Therese as they sat at the table where Therese used to sit with her father to watch the deer, chipmunks, and wild horses that came out at sunset.

"So, what did Morpheus say to you, exactly?" Hestie was asking.

"The gods are fighting," Hermie replied. "And Mom and Dad are in danger. I think he said we all are."

Therese held her breath.

"Let's both pray to him tonight and see if we can find out more," Hestie suggested.

Then Lynn spoke up. "You're in danger? And why would you *pray* to Morpheus?"

Lynn had met Morpheus many times when he'd visited in human form, and she knew he was their cousin.

"Uh, um," Hermie stuttered. "Lynn. I didn't hear you follow us out."

"It's a video game," Hestie said.

"Why are you lying to me?" Lynn insisted. "Why are you in danger?"

"It's cold out here. Don't you guys want to come inside?" It was Bobby.

"Lynn overheard us talking about Morpheus," Hermie said. "We don't know what to say."

"Why would the twins *pray* to your nephew?" Lynn asked.

"I don't think they meant *pray* literally," Bobby said. "That's a new slang word. People say, 'I'll pray to you later,' and what they mean is, 'I'll text you later.'"

"Hmm," Lynn said—and it sounded to Therese like she wasn't buying it. "But you still haven't said why you're in danger."

Therese realized the time had come for Lynn to know the truth. It wasn't fair for the adults to keep putting their children in these sticky situations.

***

Thanatos watched on helplessly as Carol, Richard, and Therese told Lynn about his family. They'd waited until after the Sterns had left, though it would have been nice to have had Bobby's help.

"This is a lame joke," Lynn said.

"It's not a joke," Carol said gently. "Look, I understand how you feel. It was hard for your father and me to believe it at first, too."

"We should have told you sooner," Richard added. "But we didn't know how."

Therese put a hand on Lynn's shoulder. "And we didn't want to hurt your relationship with Hermie and Hestie."

Lynn was taller than Therese and the same height as Hestie. Her hair was curlier than theirs, and darker, as was her skin, but she shared their same facial features—pouty lips, green eyes, slender nose, and dimples. "You really expect me to believe that Than was once the god of death? His parents are Hades and Persephone? And, for a while, you were a god, too? This is crazy." Lynn collapsed on the couch beside her mother.

"It's true." Therese took the chair opposite her.

"Then why aren't you still gods?" Lynn asked.

Than sat on the arm of Therese's chair. "We gave that up so we could raise Hermie and Hestie here."

"Are they gods too?" Lynn asked.

"Demigods," Hermie said.

Lynn's eyes widened.

Than cleared his throat to buy some time to figure out how to phrase what he was about to say. He didn't want to go into too much detail, but he wanted Lynn to believe and to understand. "There was a war on Mount Olympus, and part of the peace treaty was Zeus's condition that no more gods could be made. Therese was pregnant with the twins at the time."

Hestie sat down on the couch beside Lynn. "Gods don't become immortal until they're born."

"So, we were born *mortal*," Hermie added.

Therese said, "And the only way we could be with them was for us to become mortal, too."

Than heard the subtle quiver in Therese's voice and hated that she wouldn't be anything but joyful on her birthday. He knew she missed their life among the gods. He wouldn't have guessed all those years ago, when he was first getting to know her, that she would one day long to live in the Underworld. He'd thought her love of animals and of the

Colorado mountains and of sunsets and of pine trees would make her miserable in his father's realm. He'd been wrong.

"My best friend, Jen Holt, married Than's brother, Hip," Therese said. "Hypnos. He's the god of sleep. Jen became the goddess of abused children. And they have a son named Morpheus, the god of dreams."

"The Sterns and Bobby know about the gods," Hestie explained.

"Pete Holt is married to our Aunt Tizzie," Hermie put in.

"Wait, what?" Lynn asked. "I thought Pete Holt was dead."

Therese glanced up at Than, who inwardly groaned.

Hermie's face turned red. "Oops."

"He took over my duties as Death," Than explained. "I gave him my immortality."

"So, Pete isn't *dead*, he's *Death*," Lynn repeated. "And he's married to Tizzie. And she's, what? The goddess of death?"

"Um," Hestie looked to Therese for help.

"She's a Fury," Therese said.

Than covered his mouth in frustration. He didn't want to overwhelm the poor girl.

"A Fury?" Lynn repeated. "You mean, like the avengers of hell?"

"She's a lot nicer in person," Hermie said.

Than could almost see the wheels turning in poor Lynn's head. He really hoped the conversation wouldn't lead to the two red birds who were perched outside near the window.

Lynn scratched her head. "So, if Zeus said there could be no more gods while you were pregnant with the twins, how could Jen and— what's her husband's name?"

"Hypnos," Than said.

"Hip for short," Hermie added.

"How could Jen and Hip's child be a god and not yours?" Lynn asked Therese.

"It's a long story," Therese replied. "But, basically, they had leverage."

Lynn furrowed her brows. "So, let me get this straight. Than's parents are the rulers of the Underworld."

"Yes, sweetheart," Carol said.

"And all those gods in the stories you've told to me—they all exist? Like Zeus and Athena and Aphrodite and Poseidon? They're all real?"

"Yes," Therese said.

"What about Santa Claus and the tooth fairy? Are they real, too?"

"Why are you so angry?" Richard asked Lynn.

"Because you've been lying to me all my life."

Carol put an arm around her. "I'm so sorry, sweetheart. Can you forgive us?"

"Just tell me this." Lynn turned to Hestie. "Why is your family in danger?"

"In danger?" Carol repeated, her eyes suddenly wide with worry.

"It was just a dream," Hermie said. "We don't know if any of it's real."

"I'm sure it's nothing," Therese said, but Than knew she was lying.

***

During the drive home from their grandparents' house, Hermie wasn't surprised when his mother turned from the front passenger seat and said, "Tell me what's going on with Morpheus."

"Um, we don't know," Hermie said. "We're going to ask him tonight."

"Maybe it's time," their dad said to their mom.

"Time for what?" Hestie asked.

"Let's talk inside," their mother said.

Hermie sighed. "How long is this going to take? I made plans to meet with my friends online at nine o'clock."

"You made plans on Mom's birthday?" Hestie chided.

"I asked her first," Hermie replied. "Mom said we'd be home between eight and eight-thirty, and when I asked if we were doing anything after that, she said no."

"This is important," their father said, as he pulled the truck into their gravel drive and headed for the garage.

"So is my game. I made a commitment to my team to be there. It's World of Warcraft. I'm the tank. They'll die without me."

"This might be more important," Hestie said gently.

"This game is important to me and my friends. They're counting on me. I don't like to let people down. The talk can wait, can't it? We'll be finished by ten or ten thirty."

"We've waited sixteen years." His mom unfastened her safety belt. "We can wait another couple of hours."

Hermie tried not to let the guilt bother him as he played, but he failed, and his whole team died after an hour into the game. At least it hadn't been a total waste. They'd had fun while it had lasted, and he hadn't let them down in that.

His family was waiting for him in the living room. Apparently, they'd begun without him. He fell into one of two armchairs across from the sofa, where his parents sat frowning, with Clifford and Noodle in their laps. Hestie was already in the other armchair with Kitty, and the expression on his sister's face could only be described as perplexed.

"What did I miss?" Hermie asked.

As an answer, his canary, Chidori, chirped from her cage, "You have a destiny."

Of course, only he and Hestie heard it. To his parents, Chidori's tweets were unintelligible.

"An important destiny," Chidori chirped again.

Hermie's Grampa Hades had told him years ago that he had a destiny, so it was no surprise. Even if he had no idea what that destiny was or how he was to fulfill it, he hadn't thought much about it. It was

Hermie's belief that it would happen, whether he tried to do anything about it or not. The Fates were never wrong.

His father raked a hand through his dark, wavy hair. "When you were still a baby, Apollo had a vision of you two when you came to be about the age you are now."

"Is it safe to say this out loud?" his mother interrupted.

His father shifted on the couch. "They need to know. I'll make it quick."

His mom nodded—reluctantly it seemed to Hermie.

"So, what was the vision?" Hestie asked.

"Apollo saw you with Prometheus," their father replied.

Hermie cleared his throat, trying to hide the skepticism in his voice. "The Titan who made humankind?"

"That's right," his mother said. "And he also gave us fire against Zeus's wishes, because he loved his creation more than the gods."

Hestie stroked Kitty. "I've always thought that was pretty cool."

"But to Zeus, it was a betrayal. As punishment, Prometheus was chained to a mountain," his father said. "And Zeus's eagle ate out his liver every morning."

"And the liver grew back every evening," Hermie said. "We already know the story."

"And you know that Hercules set him free?" their mother asked.

Hestie and Hermie nodded.

"Where is he now?" Hermie asked.

"No one knows," his father said. "He went into hiding centuries ago."

"Did Apollo say why Prometheus was with *us*?" Hestie asked.

"No." Their mother helped Clifford down from her lap. "We don't know if *he* comes to *you*, or *you* find *him*."

"Obviously, *he* comes to *us*," Hermie said. "Right? We have no idea where he is."

"Nothing in this is obvious, Son," his father said. "And you need to know about another, much older, prophecy."

"Is this the one you told me about tonight, while Hermie was playing his game?" Hestie asked.

"Yes," their mother said.

His father helped Noodle, who wanted to follow Clifford, from his lap. "It's one that Prometheus told Zeus, while he was still Zeus's prisoner."

Hestie brushed her long hair from her eyes. "He said that Metis would have a son by Zeus, and that son would one day overthrow him."

"That's why Zeus swallowed Metis in the first place, and why Athena later had to be let out by Hephaestus and his ax," Hermie said.

"And then, centuries later, why Metis had to be rescued by the Athena Alliance," Hestie added.

"That's right," their father said.

"I know the story, but I didn't know Prometheus was the one who told Zeus," Hermie admitted.

"There's more," Hestie said. "When we were only a year old, Metis disguised herself as Hera and tricked Zeus. She got pregnant using dark magic."

"With a son?" Hermie asked.

"We don't know for sure," their mother said, "but that's what the Olympians suspect."

"Metis disappeared after the Olympians imprisoned Uranus for trying to wage war on them," their father went on.

"Uranus took over his father's body and nearly swallowed your Uncle Hip," their mother explained.

Their father added, "Zeus probably fears that her son and Prometheus will team up to take over the throne."

"Why would Prometheus do that?" Hermie asked. "You said he cares more about us than the gods."

"I wouldn't have suspected him if it weren't for Apollo's vision," their father said.

"Maybe Prometheus tries to stop Metis's son," Hestie offered.

"Maybe," their mother said. "The point is, we don't know where he stands. We only know that one day soon, the two of you will be in his company—whether as his prisoners or his allies, we just don't know. We need you to train."

"We shouldn't have waited this late," their father said.

"Time got away from us," their mother added. "We've been so busy. If I hadn't overheard you tonight at Grammie's talking about Morpheus, we probably would have put this off until it was too late."

"We may have already," their father said. "Don't make any plans tomorrow. We need to teach you two how to fight."

"You've been teaching us our whole lives," Hestie pointed out.

"We know how to use a sword and shield," Hermie added.

"You even taught us how to wrestle," Hestie said.

"How to punch, how to kick. What more is there?" Hermie asked.

"We never taught you how to kill," their father said.

Eva Pohler is a *USA Today* bestselling author of over thirty novels in multiple genres, including mysteries, thrillers, and young adult paranormal romance based on Greek mythology. Her books have been described as "addictive" and "sure to thrill"—*Kirkus Reviews.*

To learn more about Eva and her books, and to sign up to hear about new releases, and sales, please visit her website at www.evapohler.com.

www.ingramcontent.com/pod-product-compliance
Lightning Source LLC
Chambersburg PA
CBHW051203220726
48293CB00013B/922